DANGEROUS FRIENDSHIP

Before she went out to South Africa to stay with friends, Lena hadn't much liked the sound of their neighbour, the daunting Kane Westbrook. But before she had known him long she realized that her first impressions had been wrong ones, and in fact a friendship began to grow up between the two of them. It was a friendship that could be dangerous ...

Books you will enjoy
by ANNE HAMPSON

AUTUMN TWILIGHT

Lauren met the mysterious and disturbingly attractive Don Ramón Cabrera y Molina at her engagement party—when he lost no time in telling her that she was making a mistake and that she did not really love her fiancé. Furthermore, he added, he himself was the right man for her! What was Lauren supposed to do about it all, though?

REAP THE WHIRLWIND

Kari had not expected her father to leave her anything, least of all a half share in a hotel in Switzerland. But she went out there, nevertheless, to see what it was all about—and promptly found herself at loggerheads with the owner of the *other* half of her inheritance, the difficult Paul von Hasler!

WHERE THE SOUTH WIND BLOWS

Melanie had lost the two men she loved to her glamorous, unscrupulous sister Romaine—and she had vowed that no man should ever have the chance to break her heart again. But, against her better judgment, she found herself falling in love yet again—and once more, Romaine promptly turned up to do her usual mischief . . .

FLAME OF FATE

It was years since Alana had seen Conon Mavilis, although she knew he still hated her for having turned him down. Now, in Greece, they had met again, and Conon, smouldering and embittered, was insisting that she become his wife. And this time he had the power to make her agree . . .

DANGEROUS FRIENDSHIP

BY

ANNE HAMPSON

MILLS & BOON LIMITED

17–19 FOLEY STREET

LONDON W1A 1DR

First published 1976
This edition 1976

ISBN 0 263 71980 4

Made and Printed in Great Britain by
Richard Clay (The Chaucer Press), Ltd., Bungay, Suffolk

CHAPTER ONE

LENA RIDGEWAY frowned at her appearance as, glancing in the cracked mirror over the kitchen sink, she noted the dullness of her eyes, the lank strands of hair, the pale drawn cheeks and the lips that lacked colour.

Was it only three years ago that she had been declared the winner of a beauty competition? It had only been a local affair, it was true, but her laughing brown eyes, the russet glory of her gleaming hair, the delicately contoured cheeks with their healthy peach-bloom colour, the rosy mouth, full and generous . . . all these had compounded to produce a picture which the judges had described as 'perfect feminine attractiveness' and she had won the prize.

And now . . .

She began to hurry through the washing, taking out numerous small garments from the machine and rinsing them in the sink before putting them into the spin-dryer. It was Sunday, the day her three young step-brothers went over to their aunt's home, so affording Lena an opportunity to take a little leisure. Leisure! she thought bitterly. For the past eight months she had not known one single hour's leisure.

However, this was one occasion on which she was to have something rather pleasant in her life; she was entertaining to tea an old school-friend who, eighteen months ago, had married a South African and had gone to live on his farm in the eastern part of the Transvaal. June and Gerald were over on holiday, and as Lena had come high on their visiting list, she was one of the first of June's friends to be called on. Lena had been busy for the whole of the previous afternoon, leaving John and Billie and James to play in the garden. This morning she had made a salad, and a trifle, had baked cakes and biscuits, and when at half-past two she began laying the table in the small dining-room, she was smiling happily, for the result of her efforts was most rewarding, the table looking daintily attractive, with red roses, snow-white cloth and gleaming cutlery.

'And now to make myself look pretty!' She went upstairs to take a bath, saw that the children had played havoc with the room that morning, and so after tidying up she had little time to spend on her appearance. In her letters to June, Lena had deliberately omitted much of what had taken place in her life during the past months. She and June had been close friends since early childhood and, fully aware that June would be filled both with deep anxiety and wrathful indignation if she revealed the drastic changes that had recently occurred, Lena had not confided very much at all. But now, as she darted a look in the dressing-table mirror, she strongly suspected that the observant June would notice the difference in her appearance—and demand to be given the reason for it.

Lena herself, musing over the events which had caused the changes in her life, could not help, as always, becoming enmeshed in a web of deep depression. It had all resulted from her father's decision to marry Freda, a woman whom he had known only a few weeks. She had been left a widow with three children under four and Lena suspected that it was pity rather than love which had prompted her father to offer marriage to the woman. Lena did not particularly like her, though she naturally kept this dislike to herself. Nor was she at all enamoured with the children, who seemed particularly spoiled and naughty. The change also palled; it was no longer possible to come home and eat a quiet, well-cooked meal with her father—sometimes in the glow of the firelight, and at other times with the spring or summer sunshine streaming through the window. All that was gone; in its place was work, work and even more work.

And then the most unforeseen and terrible thing happened. Her father and stepmother were killed instantly when a coach collided with their car.

Left with the three children, Lena had asked their aunt to have them, and while this aunt had not refused outright, she had procrastinated so long that in the end Lena had given up her work and she and the children were now living on the pension paid to her by the firm for whom her father had worked at the time of his death. In Lena's life now there was no light, no hope of anything that could change her existence. Marriage was out, for no man would be willing to take on three unruly children—especially children who were not even related to the girl who was taking care of them.

'You owe them nothing,' Lena's solicitor had said at the time of her father's death, but her response had been,

'There isn't anyone else to take care of them.'

Her reverie being broken by the chiming of the clock downstairs, Lena began with more urgency to brush her hair, her attention still more on her features than anything else.

'A little extra colour to my cheeks,' she decided. 'It'll cover up the lines—— Oh, heavens, here they are!' she exclaimed as the front door bell rang. 'They're early!'

She sped downstairs and a moment later she and June were hugging one another, while Gerald, looking as if he would rather be anywhere in the world than here, merely stood by and waited for the emotional scene to come to an end.

'Oh, but it's marvellous to see you again!' Lena gestured and her friends entered the long narrow hallway. 'First on the left—but you should know! You've been in this house so many times!' After closing the door Lena followed June and Gerald into the sitting-room. 'Eighteen months since you were married and went away!'

'It's gone so quickly! You made the most beautiful chief bridesmaid any girl could have...' June's voice faded, and even Gerald was staring at Lena's drawn countenance. 'Is something wrong?' inquired June anxiously even before she had handed her coat to Lena who was waiting to take it from her. 'You did write to say your father had died, but that was some time ago——'

'Sit down, June, and I'll tell you a little about it.' Taking note, not only of her friend's expression, but also of the troubled look in Gerald's compassionate eyes, Lena realized at once that some explanation on her part would be expected. 'It's been rather hard since Father died.' She left the room, hung up the coats, then returned. 'I thought we'd eat about five—but meanwhile I'll make a pot of tea——'

'In a few minutes,' interrupted June in that customary forceful manner which Lena remembered of old. 'You look terrible, Lena—— No, it's not tactful of me, or polite, but be damned to etiquette! You know me—I've always said what I meant. What's amiss?' she added without further preamble.

Lena hesitated a moment, but then, because of the way she felt, so tired and depressed, with the whole of her future seeming to be blighted by the circumstances into which she had been plunged, she talked to her friend without the reserve which, initially, she had meant to adopt. A few interruptions came both from June and Gerald, but for the most part they listened, their changing expressions far more revealing than anything which the spoken word could convey.

'You're troubled about me,' ended Lena with deep regret. 'I didn't want you to be, June, and that's why I didn't put much in my letters.'

'Much?' echoed June accusingly. 'You put precious little! Apart from telling me your father had died in an accident you said nothing!'

Lena bit her lip, feeling guilty.

'I didn't want you to worry, June. After all, you'd only just been married; it wasn't for me to burden you with my troubles.'

'*Just* been married? We've been married over a year and a half!'

'At the time it was all happening, I mean.' Swiftly Lena rose and said she would make that pot of tea. 'I'll not be long,' she added, and went to the door.

'Getting out of the way, eh?' grimly from June. 'Well, we'll discuss it when you come back! Something's got to be done—this whole business sorted out—and little June here's the very one to do it!'

Lena, standing by the door, shook her head dejectedly.

'Nothing can be done, June. I'm stuck with these three children until they are old enough to look after themselves.'

'That'll not be for ten years or more! What about you—and your lost youth? You're already twenty-four, Lena; it's time you were looking around for a husband. Doesn't this aspect of it ever enter your head?'

'Of course it does; it's only natural.' Lena half turned away, her eyes shading as she recalled the many occasions when her mind would lose itself in a delightful mist of imagination. Her ideal man would appear then—tall and dark and handsome—and she would see herself married in a lovely white creation similar to that which June had worn; she would go off to some exotic place for a honeymoon; she and her handsome husband would return to the little nest which they had previously made for themselves.

'Well then, why don't you do something about it?'

Lena looked hopelessly at her.

'There isn't anything I can do,' she said, and went from the room to the kitchen to make the pot of tea. About ten minutes later she returned with the tray on which was the tea and three cups and saucers. She poured the tea and handed a cup to each of her guests. And all the while not one word passed any of their lips. Looking at last from June to Gerald, Lena frowned a little to herself, wondering just what they had been saying while she was out of the room. She was soon to know.

'We want you to come back with us for a holiday.' It was Gerald who spoke in his quiet and placid voice which was very different in tone from that of his wife.

'A *long* holiday!' inserted June, and her husband nodded his head in instant agreement.

A faint and bitter smile touched Lena's lips.

'It's kind of you both, and I do appreciate your offer, but I can't leave these children. They have no one else——'

'Where are they now?' demanded June, although she had already been informed that they were with their aunt. Lena repeated this, adding in answer to a further question from June that this aunt was the sister of the children's mother. 'This aunt must take them——' began June, when Lena interrupted her.

'She has a child of her own, June.'

'So these make four. It's her problem, not yours.'

But Lena was shaking her head.

'It's no use, June. I can't leave them.'

'Do you love them?'

'Strangely, I don't. They're unattractive children, all of them. I have a dreadful time——' She stopped abruptly, not for one moment having intended saying anything like that.

'Lena,' said Gerald seriously, his tea going cold on the small table at his elbow where he had placed it, 'these children are not your responsibility. As June says, your entire youth is going to be lost. It's neither fair nor necessary that you accept responsibility for their upbringing. It isn't as if even one of them was your father's. None of them is a blood relation.'

'They'll not thank you, when they grow up, for the sacrifices you've made,' interposed June angrily. 'No, Lena, you must take our advice and wash your hands of them. Gerald and I talked while you were in the kitchen and we both came to the same conclusion—that you must get right away; if you don't you're not going to be able to rid yourself of the encumbrance. This aunt—what a let-out for her! She must be thanking her stars that you're such a fool as to take on the responsibility of her sister's children.'

'I don't think their aunt would have them——' Lena shook her head. 'No, I'm sure she wouldn't.'

'Then they must go into a foster home.'

'I couldn't...' But suddenly Lena's voice trailed away as she put a hand to her head. These violent pains had begun about five months ago, and recently they recurred with what was becoming rather alarming frequency.

'What's wrong?' Sharply June spoke, her green eyes glinting, hard and wrathful. 'A headache?'

Lena nodded and rose from the chair.

'I'm sorry ... I'll get an aspirin——'

'Nerves!' declared June. 'Oh, but I'm furious about all this!'

Although the tea was a most pleasant meal, with light conversation taking place between the three sitting at the table, Lena sensed June's anger and the concern of her husband. She sighed inwardly, sorry that this afternoon to which she had so looked forward was being somewhat marred by the revelations which were having so marked an effect on her friends.

And it did not help at all when Mrs Poulton, the children's aunt, brought them back sooner than was usual.

'We've had some friends call unexpectedly,' said Mrs Poulton when Lena answered her knock at the back door. 'So I hope you don't mind my bringing them a little before their time?'

An agonizing pain shot through Lena's head as disappointment flooded over her.

'But, Mrs Poulton,' she protested, almost ready to cry, 'I also have friends. They've come to tea—and we haven't even finished——'

'Well, it's almost six o'clock.'

'You usually bring them at half-past seven, Mrs Poulton.'

'I've just said,' returned the woman impatiently, 'that we've got visitors...' Her voice trailed away and Lena turned to see June standing behind her, fury both in the compression of her mouth and the glint in her eyes.

'I'm terribly sorry about this, June——' Lena broke off as Billie, racing past her, slid on the carpet and, falling, set up a deafening howl. 'I'll take them to the kitchen while you and Gerald finish your tea.' James, his face dirty and his nose requiring the urgent use of a handkerchief, clung to Lena's freshly washed dress with fingers from which he had just licked the remains of a bar of chocolate.

'I want a drink!' he cried peevishly. 'Auntie Norah

wouldn't give me one. She said I'd have one when I got home!'

'I want one as well...' Lena heard no more. The pain in her head was suddenly excruciating and without warning everything went black and had not Gerald, appearing conveniently upon the scene, leapt forward to catch her, there was no knowing what injuries she might have sustained, for she would have fallen against the corner of the electric cooker. Gerald carried her to the sitting-room and she came round almost immediately he put a glass of water to her lips.

'Oh ... what happened——?' She stopped abruptly, hearing her friend's wrathful voice.

'Miss Ridgeway happens to be ill, Mrs—Mrs——?'

'Poulton—but you see, we have visitors——'

'All I can see at the moment, madam, is that you must take these children back to your house—and keep them there! Miss Ridgeway is in no way responsible for them, and as she'll be seeing the doctor first thing in the morning, she obviously can't be bothered with them—— Here, you—Jimmy or Billie or whatever you're called—outside!'

'Why, you——!' Mrs Poulton seemed to be lost for words. 'I——'

'And this other little brat—— Yes, I've got him by the scruff of the neck! Outside! Off with you all! Your auntie is taking you back to her house——' Then there was a loud bang as the door was closed.

'Well,' declared June when her husband joined her, 'that was rather profitable. What an obnoxious bunch of brats they turned out to be! How's Lena?'

'Coming round.'

'Really, June,' protested Lena trying to sit up, 'you can't do that. I've agreed to have them——'

'Signed anything?'

'No——'

'It wouldn't matter if you had. You're ill—ready to succumb to a nervous breakdown. And as you've no relatives, I'm taking charge. Gerald doesn't object, do you, darling?'

'Most certainly not. You have all my support.' Although far less forceful than his wife, Gerald was equally determined to do something for Lena.

'I'm staying with Lena tonight,' June told her husband. 'Will you convey my apologies to Mum and tell her what's happened? She's always thought a lot of Lena and she wouldn't want me to leave her at a time like this.'

Lena opened her mouth to protest, then closed it again. She was so tired and lethargic that at this moment nothing was more appealing to her than to relax and allow her friend to deal with the situation in any way she thought best. As this was running through her mind a sharp 'rat-tat' was heard. This time it was Gerald who insisted on going to the door.

His quiet voice reached the two girls in the sitting-room.

'No, Mrs Poulton, there isn't a chance of their coming back tonight—or tomorrow, for that matter. Our friend, Miss Ridgeway, is in no fit condition to take care of them. I suggest that, if you yourself are unwilling to have them, you get in touch with the local authority, who will take the children into their care——'

'You're suggesting that my poor dead sister's innocent babes should go into a home! Oh, what kind of a man are you! I've never heard of anything so wicked and unfeeling!'

'You don't want them to go into care?' Still the voice was quiet, and unhurried. June, aware that she herself would have handled the woman very differently, gave a grimace, which presently progressed to a laugh. 'In that case, Mrs Poulton, you'll prefer to have them yourself. Now, that is most considerate and dutiful in you——'

'I have my own child, and a husband. Miss Ridgeway has no one but herself to think about!'

'That's absolutely true—from now on, Mrs Poulton. I believe my friend told you that we hadn't finished our tea? So you'll understand if I bid you good evening—I *am* bidding you good evening, Mrs Poulton, so you needn't interrupt me again. And I advise you to take your foot out of the doorway—because I assure you that I intend to close the door, and I should hate to break your ankle. Oh, and by the way ... if you come back the door will not be opened. We don't wish for any more interruptions to our meal.'

'So quiet and yet effective,' laughed June when he returned. 'Lena's feeling better, so let's go and finish those excellent goodies she prepared for us!'

The following morning June went out and rang Lena's doctor. This in spite of Lena's repeated protests that she was feeling better and that she really ought to go and collect the children.

'They're more used to me than their aunt,' she pointed out. 'I can't help feeling they'll be fretting.'

'Rubbish! Those detestable brats wouldn't know how to fret!'

Doctor Knowles, who had been given the complete picture by June while Lena was upstairs, having decided to make the beds, looked gravely at Lena and said outright that she was in no fit condition to care for the three boys.

'Even if they were your own I should recommend that you go into hospital for a rest cure,' he said sternly when Lena would have made a protest. 'Your friend here has told me of her invitation; I strongly advise you to accept it, Lena.' He had known her a long while and had always used her Christian name. 'I did warn you, a few months ago when you called at the surgery with one of the children, that you were heading for trouble. This is a mental problem as well as the physical strain that's entailed by having the children. Both consciously and subconsciously you are resentful; you're perpetually aware that your life is being sacrificed—and for children that have no claim on you whatsoever. Had they been your father's children you would have owed them something; you owe absolutely nothing to the children of a woman, now dead, who was a total stranger to you until a year ago.'

'It was all very logical,' Lena was agreeing when the doctor, having extracted from Lena the promise that she would accept her friend's invitation, had left the house, 'but I have a most uncomfortable feeling of guilt. Somehow, I feel that I'm letting my father down. You see, June, he intended to take those children under his wing; he would have expected me to accept the responsibility for them.'

'I don't believe that your father, who thought so much about you, would have wished you to sacrifice your entire youth to strangers. Why, even I can remember his repeatedly saying he wished you could find a boy you could begin going steady with because he'd like to see you married before anything happened to him.'

Lena nodded; she was once again feeling lethargic; vaguely she knew she was being driven into a situation which was not of her own choosing, but she had to own that it was most pleasant to allow someone else to make these plans which all she had to do was follow—without even exerting a modicum of energy. South Africa ... a farm. She had always imagined what it must be like to live in the country, away from the crowds and the noise, but she had never imagined herself taking a holiday in a place so attractive as South Africa. How long would she stay with June and Gerald? They had both said, last evening before Gerald left, that she must stay for just as long as she liked.

'I might become so enamoured with your country that I shan't want to return,' she warned, but the answer she received was to the effect that such a decision would not come amiss, since she had no real ties in England.

As June and Gerald were not returning to Africa for another three weeks, June insisted that Lena should stay with her parents.

'That's not really necessary, June,' said Lena as she and June sat over a cup of coffee half an hour after the doctor's visit. 'I shall be all right here. I've to gather a suitable wardrobe together, and this is best done on my own.'

'You can still do it on your own if you live with us. No, you can't stay here, Lena, simply because that dreadful woman will bring those kids back.'

'I've no need to take them.' What a relief it was not to have them, thought Lena. Any ordinary morning she would have been running around after them—attending to their wants, or trying to stop one or the other of them screaming for something he could not have. There would be the beds to make, the breakfast dishes to wash, the children to get ready and take out with her if she happened to have some shopping to do. This sitting here with her friend in the peace and quietness of a tidy room was sheer bliss, and already a bloom had settled on her cheeks, cheeks that had been pale for months. But her general appearance was by no means satisfactory; she was drawn and, during the past months, she had lost so much weight that most of her clothes hung drably on her thin figure.

'What will you do with the house?' June spoke after a short silence; Lena knew at once that she had changed the subject deliberately, hoping that Lena would have time to consider her proposal and eventually come to the conclusion that she would, after all, be better staying with June's parents until her departure for South Africa. 'Will you let it while you're away?'

'Perhaps that would be best,' replied Lena thoughtfully. 'It wouldn't be wise to leave it empty, would it?'

'Not for any length of time,' returned June with a frown. 'You might be burgled.'

Lena nodded, but at the same time she glanced around and decided that there was not much of any value in the house. Her father had earned an excellent salary, but he had never been a thrifty man, spending his money on things which Lena often considered to be trivial.

'I ought to put it in the hands of a house agent.'

June agreed, and then asked again if Lena would come and stay with her parents. Lena nodded, having by this time decided that her friend was right when she predicted that Mrs Poulton would bring the children back. And, knowing herself, Lena feared she would feel so sorry for them that she would take them in again; in consequence she would be right back to where she was before June had arrived to rescue her from the plight into which she had been thrown by the deaths of her father and his wife.

'Yes, June, I'll come,' said Lena with a smile. 'And thanks a lot for everything.'

'No need to thank me——'

'Oh, but there is! I'd got into a rut, accepting my lot without even trying to extricate myself.'

'Well, if our presence here yesterday has helped you that's all the reward I need, Lena. As for this invitation—we shall both love having you living with us. The homestead isn't anything spectacular, but it's comfortable.'

'Is it lonely there?' asked Lena curiously. 'From your letters I seemed to gain the impression that it was.'

'It's all on its own, yes. Our nearest neighbour's land adjoins ours, in that a stream divides us, but his house is about a quarter of a mile away.'

'It sounds wonderful.' Lena was already becoming enthusiastic about her forthcoming holiday. 'Can you see your neighbour's house?'

'Koranna Lodge? Yes, it stands out, not only because it's on a rise, but also because it's a very splendid place—a colonial mansion built by his great-grandfather. It's the "house of character" type, set in the most beautiful grounds with mature trees and shrubs, and with spreading lawns. In his gardens you'll find numberless flowers, like the African tulip tree, the poinsettias and hibiscus, allamandas and bougainvillaea—oh, he has so many exotic flowers that you'd need to see them to believe it!'

Lena's eyes began to shine. She loved flowers; she loved trees even more.

'You're friendly with these people?'

'People? There's only Kane—Kane Westbrook. He's a bachelor—not much time for women at all from what I've gathered since knowing him. Yes, we're friendly—although not intimately so. He's a jolly helpful neighbour, but there's an aloofness about him that's rather difficult to penetrate. You never feel totally at ease with him. He seems——' June stopped, reflecting for a space. 'He seems far superior to us; we're the plebians and he the patrician—if you know what I mean,' she added with a deprecating little laugh.

'You've made your meaning very clear indeed,' returned Lena, and there was a grim edge to her voice. 'He sounds as if he's a snob.'

'No, you're wrong! Oh, dear, I've given you a totally wrong impression of him, I'm afraid. He's one of those people you would like to have for a close friend but who, because of this aloofness, will not allow you to become quite that intimate. It's as if he's willing for you to go so far, but you mustn't go too far.' June looked at Lena, a faintly anxious expression in her green eyes. 'I still haven't conveyed a true picture of Kane, have I?'

Lena hesitated, loath to say anything at all about a man she had not yet met.

'I feel I shall be afraid of him,' was her frank admission at last.

June laughed.

'I was like that with him at first, so I can't honestly say you won't be, can I?'

'*You* were afraid?' Lena shot her a disbelieving glance. 'I've never known you to be afraid of anyone!'

'There aren't many people who can intimidate me,' June had to own. 'But Kane has a way of—well, putting you in your place if, by some spontaneous act or remark, you happen to forget it.'

Lena said nothing; the picture she was forming was not too attractive. This Kane Westbrook appeared to be a man with whom one must always be on one's guard, taking care not to put a foot out of place, as it were. Oh, well, she would not be having much to do with him so she had nothing to fear.

'He sounds wealthy,' she remarked at last, just for something to say, as the conversation had languished.

June nodded her head. The sunlight caught her

auburn curls and they shone. Lena was reminded of the time when she, too, had hair that shone—healthy hair, not lifeless and dull as it was now.

'He's as rich as a nabob! Has hordes of Africans working on his estate, and no less than four servants in the house. It's a large place, though, so he needs four servants.'

'Tell me about your house,' invited Lena, much more interested in Mtula Farm than the imposing mansion belonging to this Kane Westbrook. Lena liked small houses, not great barns which were cold and unfriendly, as she was sure Koranna Lodge must be.

'It's rambling but unlovely, made of corrugated iron with a thatched roof. In the kitchen there's an enormous cooking stove.'

'Don't you have electricity?'

'Not yet. It's rather nice, though, to use oil lamps and candles.'

'Yes,' murmured Lena, 'I expect it is.' She paused a moment, her big eyes becoming dreamy. 'Tell me about your garden, and the farm.'

'We don't have a great deal of time to bother about the garden, unfortunately. However, we do have some flowers...' She paused, her glance darting to her friend's face. 'You've always loved gardening. So if you want to do some...?'

'I shall adore doing it!' exclaimed Lena. 'June, I'm going to enjoy this holiday no end!'

'I sincerely hope so.' Another pause and then, 'As for our farm—it's mixed, as I said. We grow oats and maize, and we keep sheep and cattle. It's a neat farm, and well run, because it's been in Gerald's family for about twenty-five years; but it's just an allotment in comparison to Koranna.'

This brought a slight frown to Lena's forehead.

'I'm quite sure that I'll be far more thrilled with Mtula Farm than with the pretentious colonial mansion belonging to your arrogant neighbour.'

'Oh, dear,' sighed June but with a hint of wry humour in her voice, 'I *have* given you a bad impression of Kane. He's charming, really.'

The 'really' seemed to qualify the word charming—at least, to Lena's ears, but she refrained from saying anything more about the 'patrician', as June had termed him. His house was a quarter of a mile distant from Mtula Farm and, as Lena had already predicted, she would see little or nothing of him during her stay with June and her husband.

CHAPTER TWO

OVER the silent bushveld lay the shimmering heat of the midday sun, which shone down mercilessly from an azure sky. Reclining on the back stoep, a book on her knee, Lena allowed her thoughts to wander back to the day of her arrival in South Africa. The weeks prior to her departure had been somewhat hectic, her having to contact the house agent, and then rearrange the furnishings of the house so that she could safely lock away in one room all those items which she did not wish to include in the general furnishings of her home. June had helped her with this task, but Lena, reminding her that she had many friends and relatives yet to visit, refused to accept any assistance with the garden which, Lena felt, must be weeded and made to look attractive for the prospective tenants who would be taking over the house during her absence.

'I thought I'd have oceans of time!' she was exclaiming when, with only three days to go before her departure, she had still not bought all that she considered necessary for her holiday in a hot country. 'I feel I haven't anywhere near enough cotton dresses and blouses.'

'I've a sewing machine,' June told her soothingly, 'and you can buy dress materials in Fonteinville—that's our nearest town, where we shop and find entertainment. If you're short of everyday clothes then you can easily make some.'

That was true, so Lena relaxed, feeling that to rush around the way she had been doing was more than a little stupid; she had no desire to arrive at the farm feeling as tired as when she had had the children living with her.

Excitement had filled Lena when the actual day of departure arrived. She had never flown, and the great VC 10 which took her and her friends to Johannesburg was in itself a treat. The flight was smooth and pleasant; Johannesburg itself, when she at last looked down upon it, was disappointing, with its dark and smoky evidence of mining activities, its high-rise buildings and its 'peas-in-a-pod' houses, appearing from this height to be of matchbox proportions.

The plane's touch-down had been easy, the ensuing formalities conducted without fuss, and then had come the journey by car to Mtula Farm, a journey that had been interrupted by a night's stay at Risdstad, a small town about half-way between Johannesburg and Fonteinville.

Lena recalled her first glimpse of the house in which she was to live; unpretentious and sprawling, it was at the same time warm and inviting. And as she sat here now, in the cool of the stoep, she allowed her eyes to wander over the house and garden. 'Home is what you make it', her grandmother so often used to repeat, and never was that more true than at Mtula Farm. June was a homemaker; she had a flair for decor, for the blending of colours; she seemed to have an especial insight as to how a certain piece of furniture or bric-à-brac would look in a certain corner, or room. With her limited means she had created a veritable palace within the austere walls of the house. Almost unconsciously Lena allowed her eyes to wander to the colonial mansion on the rise, its white walls gleaming in the sunshine. June talked a good deal about the owner of Koranna Lodge, but as yet Lena had not met him. Not that she had any desire to do so; the man seemed too superior for her liking. The house, though, was the most attractive Lena had ever seen. Even from this distance it arrested the attention, and when, having strolled to the stream one day, Lena had managed to get a closer view, she had just stood and gasped in admiration. From the main road itself the house was not visible, but its high wrought-iron gates and supporting granite pillars provided the evidence that a home of some elegance lay at the end of the long avenue of ancient oak trees which lined the drive.

'Sleeping?' June's soft voice broke into Lena's reverie and she turned her head, a smile leaping to her lips.

'No—just day-dreaming,' she murmured, moving her rattan chair a little in order to make room for June to pass and take possession of another chair. June flopped down and gave a long contented sigh.

'I adore it here. Do you know, Lena, I haven't yet got over the novelty of living in this hot and beautiful land!'

'I can understand that,' returned Lena with feeling. 'It's the peace, for one thing, that appeals to me. But there's the sunshine as well, and the scenery...' Her voice trailed off as her eyes found the clear outline of the mountains. Massive against the crystalline sky, they formed a rather awe-inspiring backcloth for the lovely white mansion standing on its hill. Sweeping away to the west was a spectacular valley, with grassy slopes and plains on which thousands of Kane Westbrook's sheep grazed. Away in another direction stretched the veld, still shimmering under the ruthless heat of this, the hottest part of the day. On the veld vegetation was often sparse, but here and there were scattered thorny mimosas, while willows fringed the banks of what few tributary streams there were. Prickly pear and the milk bush sometimes relieved the parched aspect of the landscape, and over by a meander of the river was a large copse of blue-gum trees.

'I'm glad you're liking it here,' from June in tones edged with relief. 'Gerald and I did wonder if the heat would get you, or whether the continuous profusion of the sun itself might prove too much for you.'

'I love the sun! I'm feeling a lot better already,' added Lena, looking with gratitude at her friend. 'And that's only after one week!'

'You're not looking yourself, all the same,' remarked June, examining Lena's face critically. 'It'll take some time for you to recover fully from all that overwork. It wasn't as if you'd been used to it. You and your father didn't make a mess, so there was very little to do in the way of household chores.'

Allowing this to pass without comment, Lena said after a pause,

'About the garden, June—I really could get to work on it——'

'Not until you've had a thorough rest! A week's nothing, as Gerald told you last night when you began deploring your laziness, as you decided to term it. You came for a holiday, remember. If the holiday extends to a long stay, and that to permanency, then so much the better. But as yet, you're on holiday—so there'll be no gardening until you're looking healthy and strong—and a good deal more rounded,' she thought to add as her glance strayed to Lena's figure. 'Just take things easy; go for walks as you have been doing, then rest in between. I'm sorry I can't be with you all the while, but, as you know, we're two boys short and I've had to help in the fields. However, the boys are expected back tomorrow and I shall be able to spend more time with you.'

'It doesn't matter,' returned Lena at once. 'Naturally I'd love having your company, but I knew from the start that you wouldn't be able to spend all your time entertaining me. I'm perfectly content, June, I assure you. I've really enjoyed being able to read, and to just sit and relax quietly.' A frown appeared on her brow, but she did not know it. 'Sometimes it was sheer purgatory in that house—bedlam!'

June nodded sympathetically.

'Those children hadn't been brought up in the right way and that's why they were such a problem. Well, let their aunt cope with their tantrums!'

'She did say she was keeping them——' Lena shook her head. 'I rather think she'll already have changed her mind.'

'So do I.'

June remained with Lena for about half an hour; by then Lulu, the dusky housemaid, came out to say that lunch was ready. After the meal Lena went to her pretty bedroom and lay down, going off to sleep immediately, and waking up an hour later feeling totally refreshed. The sun being no longer so high in the sky, the intense heat had subsided and after having washed and put on a crisp cotton dress Lena decided to take a stroll along the river bank.

'I'll be away a couple of hours or so,' she told June, who was just going out to harrow the mealies for her husband. 'I feel like exploring the river bank.'

June smiled and nodded her approval. Then she added,

'One of Kane's boys came over while you were resting; we're all invited to a barbecue on Friday evening.'

'All? You mean I'm invited as well?'

'That's right. Gerald saw Kane in Fonteinville a couple of days ago and mentioned that we had a visitor—an old school-friend of mine. So naturally he'd include you in the invitation. I'm ever so pleased, as you'll have the opportunity of meeting a few of our far-flung neighbours and friends.' She glanced towards the mealie field. 'I'll have to go. That rain storm yesterday resulted in thousands of weeds springing up!'

So she was going to meet the 'patrician' ... Lena's feelings were mixed, since on the one hand she was apprehensive of the meeting but on the other she welcomed an evening out. June had previously mentioned a barbecue which Kane had given last year when he had friends staying with him. From June's vivid description it had been a most enjoyable affair, with everyone from miles around being invited.

Lena's musings continued as she strolled in leisurely fashion along the bank of the Klein Umgola, a pretty stream whose waters merged with several other streams before finding a final outlet to the sea via the Limpopo River. Gerald had told Lena that during the dry season the stream—and many like it—was merely a meandering line of dark green vegetation, with a chain of pools remaining, and which provided sufficient water for the requirements of the cattle. The stream was now flowing fairly strongly, the result of the thunderstorm of the previous afternoon. On its banks flame-vines and ferns grew among the sere grass, with here and there patches of prickly pear growing on the low slopes which spread in gentle undulations away from the stream.

Suddenly, through a clearing in the copse of blue-gums, Kane Westbrook's house came into view. Stately and gleaming, it seemed a most fitting place for the 'patrician' described by June, and of whom Lena had formed a picture of a man whose character was not at all attractive; this despite the protestations of June that she had unwittingly given Lena a wrong impression of her neighbour. Stopping, Lena gazed at the house, noting the large windows which were attractively shaded by blue and white striped sunblinds, the vine-covered stoep which ran along what appeared to be the back of the house, the mature trees, and the exotic colour which even from this distance could quite easily be discerned. A magnificent mansion without any doubt, decided Lena and, for some strange reason, she found herself actually looking forward to meeting the owner—which of course she would be doing quite soon, at the barbecue to which she had been invited.

Moving on again, Lena had been walking for some minutes when, rounding a tree-fringed bend, she saw a tree-trunk lying in the water, but seeming to be still held to the bank by some of its roots. It made an inviting place to sit and without hesitation Lena stepped on to it, and after cautiously treading her way to the middle she sat down, and, taking off her shoes, dangled her feet in the stream. The soft lapping of the water was like music drifting over the still, limpid air; the sun, although hot, was no longer uncomfortably so, and in any case, the slender willows growing along the watercourse provided a welcome shade. She leant back, resting her weight on her hands, her eyes appreciating the immensity of the landscape, the harmony produced by the combination of shape and colour and the reflections of clouds in the water, while her senses absorbed the delights of the primeval solitude and the deep, deep silence into which the only intrusions were the murmuring of the stream and the occasional hum of an insect as it flew by, its wings flashing iridescent colours as the sun's brilliant rays caught them.

Time passed; the angle between earth and sun lengthening, giving an added depth to the landscape as new shades of colour appeared—every shade between pink and rose. Later, the bushveld would glow with deep crimson and gold, and, later still, the entrancing violet that precedes the deep purple of an African night.

At last, and not without some reluctance, Lena decided that it was time she began making tracks for home. She felt she could have sat here for hours and hours, but she eventually comforted herself by the reminder that there was always another day. She was about to get to her feet when, without warning, the tree moved away from the bank and began to proceed downstream, carried by the current. Not at first grasping the fact that she was in any real danger—since the speed of the tree was such that she could have jumped without difficulty on to the bank—Lena hesitated just a moment too long, being unwilling to jump on to thorny ground without first putting on her shoes. The tree gained speed; it also drifted into midstream, and now she had no chance at all of jumping on to either bank. How stupid of her not to have jumped instantly she saw what was happening! A few thorns in her feet would have been far preferable to the danger that now faced her. She thought of calling out, then abandoned the idea, since she could not possibly be heard.

'What am I to do?' she whispered fearfully. Her shoes had gone, for she needed both her hands to cling to the tree. 'If only I could swim!' The stream meandered more than ever now and she soon realized that she was actually drifting through Kane Westbrook's estate. Reaching a particularly wide meander, the log, swung right round by the increased velocity of the water, struck the bank, crushing Lena's ankle and throwing her off balance. A sharp cry of pain broke the silence before, flinging out her arms in a futile attempt to catch hold of something, she plunged into the water.

'What——?' The one word, uttered by an astounded masculine voice, fell upon Lena's ears and the next she knew was that a pair of strong arms had shot out and caught her before the current could carry her away from the bank. Hauled from the water, she managed to gasp out a spluttering,

'Oh, *thank* you!' as she stood shivering on the bank in her bare feet, a sorry figure indeed, her clothes and hair dripping with muddy water, and looked up into a pair of metallic grey eyes set in an angular sun-bitten face which she automatically knew belonged to Kane Westbrook. What a way in which to be introduced to June's neighbour! she thought, then gave a little moan as the pain in her ankle shot right up to her thigh.

'I suppose you're wondering who I am,' she began, when he interrupted her, his eyes having travelled to the foot which she was keeping off the ground.

'I conclude that you're Miss Ridgeway, the young lady who's staying with Gerald and June.' Abrupt the words, and dispassionate. 'However, this is no time for questions and answers,' he added, and before she could guess at his intention she found herself lifted right off her feet.

'Your clothes!' she protested, but Kane Westbrook made no response; he carried her across a wide sweeping lawn bordered by a luxuriance of exotic colour and perfume, and into the house, taking her straight into a bathroom where he set her down on a chair.

'You're Mr Westbrook?' Again she looked up into those metallic eyes. He merely nodded before asking her what had happened to her foot. She told him that it had been crushed between the tree-trunk and the river bank, then immediately went on to ask him to send a message over to June.

'Gerald will then come and fetch me,' she added. 'I don't want to trouble you any more——'

'Let me take a look at this foot.' Stooping, he took it in his hand; she felt the warmth, and the pressure of his fingers as they probed about, examining the bone. 'Bruised badly but not broken.'

'That's a relief. About that message——'

'It'll take time to get one of my boys from the fields. And as all my house servants have gone off to a celebration of some sort in the native village, you'll just have to accept my hospitality.' His tones, brusque and faintly arrogant, seemed to convey the message that she had somehow displeased him by her reluctance to accept his help. And, come to think of it, she had been rather ungracious in her attitude. Feeling unaccountably depressed by this unpropitious beginning, embarrassed by her appearance, and in pain from her injured ankle, she had the utmost difficulty in suppressing the tears that were gathering behind her eyes.

'I'm sorry if I offended you,' she said in a small voice. 'What have you in mind?'

'A bath first of all,' was his unhesitating reply, 'and then I'll attend to that ankle.'

'A bath...' She needed one, no doubt of that. But with her inability to put her left foot on the floor she did not see how she would manage to get into the bath. She looked into his lean unsmiling face and said, 'I don't think I'll be able to get into the bath, and in any case, I'd have to put these same clothes back on again——'

'You're shivering,' he broke in curtly. 'A hot bath's imperative. As for your clothes—I can provide you with all that's necessary. My cousin, who spends her holidays with me, leaves some of her things here.'

'But...' Lena was shaking her head, and indicating with her hand, as if to tell him once again that the injured foot was preventing her from getting into the bath.

'Get undressed, and into a towel,' he ordered imperatively. 'When you're ready I'll lift you into the bath.' Stooping, he turned on the taps. The next moment Lena was staring at the closed door, no doubts in her mind as to whether or not she should obey him. The coldly practical Mr Kane Westbrook was in no mood for listening to objections on her part.

It was a relief to rid herself of the wet clothes and to feel the warmth of the bath-sheet which, when she heard the firm tread of Kane's approaching footsteps, she wrapped securely around her damp and shivering body.

He knocked, but entered without ceremony before she had time to say come in. Over his arm he carried a clean towel which he put within her reach. Then he lifted her into the bath.

'Call me when you're ready to come out,' he said abruptly. 'I'll go and find those clothes I spoke of.'

Once again she was alone, sitting in the bath with the towel still around her.

Twenty minutes later, having bathed and also given her hair a good rinse, she called out; she was standing on one leg, the clean bath towel wrapped around her, when Kane entered carrying the clothes. He lifted her out of the bath and then, instead of disappearing immediately, he stood for a space looking at her with an impassive expression.

What was he thinking? she wondered, automatically brushing the wet strands of hair away from her face. His eyes were coldly impersonal, his lips set and unsmiling.

'When you're dressed you can call me again.' She was sitting on the chair where he had put her, the towel covering all but her toes. 'There's a clean brush and comb in the cabinet,' he thought to add as he turned to the door. 'Don't be afraid to use it; Jennifer won't mind.'

The clothing he had brought included everything she required, and Lena could not help colouring as she put on the underwear. There was a white cotton shirt-blouse and a pair of dark blue denims and, lastly, a pair of sandals. The size would once have been right for Lena, but now the clothes hung on her, being far too big.

Having found the brush and comb, she used them, but her hair was still very wet and it hung limply on to her shoulders.

However, she was warm and dry, and, apart from the pain in her ankle, she was none the worse for her frightening experience.

Reluctant to call him, she tried to put her foot down, but the pain was too much and resignedly she opened the door and called out. Kane appeared at once, lifted her up and carried her along the corridor, under an ornamental arch, and into the living-room. Here he put her on to a couch, and only then did the whole situation become unreal as, slowly, like the drifting of a cloud, the events of the past hour flitted across the edge of her mind. It seemed, as she pondered the situation in which she found herself at this moment, almost impossible that she was sitting here, in the luxury of the 'patrician's' home, having been literally carried about by him. She recalled June's description of him, mentally agreeing that it fitted. The aloofness was more than a little pronounced; added to it was an air of superiority which at this time was strengthened by the fact that he appeared to have little or no interest in Lena whatsoever, yet this impression was to fade on the instant as she saw the medicine box which he had placed on a small table, and out of which he was now taking a bandage.

'It'll be all right,' she began, feeling far from comfortable, mainly owing to the man's silence. He seemed as if he had no desire to speak to her at all. 'If you would be so kind as to take me back to Mtula Farm . . .?' She bit her lip, her discomfiture increased by the compression of his mouth. She wondered if he were always as impatient as this. He certainly meant to attend to her ankle before taking her home, and she felt thankful that she had told June that she would be a couple of hours or so. By the time she arrived back home she would have been away rather longer than the two hours but not so much longer that June would have begun to worry about her.

He sat down next to her on the couch, took her foot in his hand, examined it again and then, satisfied that she had sustained nothing more serious than a sprain, he fixed the bandage.

'And now,' he said with a sort of dignified courtesy, 'you can tell me what happened?'

She looked at him in some bewilderment for, bored and impatient as he appeared to be, he seemed in no hurry to be rid of her. His gaze was intense, penetrating; she had the sensation of being thoroughly examined . . . both in mind and body.

'I started off intending to explore the river bank,' she began, her voice low and musical, her smile hesitant, because she felt shy suddenly . . . and a little afraid of this man, just as she had predicted she would be when she had been discussing him with June. 'But then I noticed the tree-trunk; it seemed to be anchored to the bank by some of its roots and as it never occurred to me that it might move, I decided to sit on it for a while. I took off my shoes so that I could dip my feet in the water.'

Kane drew a deep breath.

'Did it not occur to you that the roots must inevitably be rotten?' he asked impatiently.

Lena shook her head, returning a meek,

'I never even gave the matter a thought.'

'How like a woman!'

Her chin lifted, but the retort that leapt to her lips

was stemmed immediately. She owed him so much—most probably her life. Also, he was the very good neighbour of Gerald and June.

'I had been there quite a while, and had just decided to step back on to the bank when the tree began to move downstream.'

He nodded his head.

'And when it reached the large meander it gathered speed. That was to be expected.'

'I suppose so.' She had felt embarrassed before; she now felt deflated. 'It was lucky for me that you happened to be at hand,' she said.

'I had just been taking a leisurely stroll around the garden; your cry reached me as I was about to return to the house.' The element of censure that had previously edged his tones was replaced by an impersonal formality. Lena strongly suspected that, had she not been the guest of his neighbour, she would have been subjected to some caustic remarks which would have made her cheeks burn. As it was, Kane Westbrook had decided to guard his tongue, in all probability remembering that she was to be his guest at the barbecue. 'If you're feeling better I'll take you back to Mtula Farm,' he offered at length. 'I believe that your ankle will be all right, but you will of course make up your own mind whether or not to see a doctor.' He went on to say that he would bring his car right up to the front of the house, and Lena, loath to have him carry her even yet again, seized on his brief absence to hop awkwardly to the door.

'You managed?' he looked surprised. 'Let me see you get into the car, then?' He sounded faintly amused, she thought, and hesitated, reluctant to make a fool of herself. 'No?' with a lift of his straight dark brows. 'You'd prefer that I assist you?' Which meant in effect that he would carry her. She looked at him, her big brown eyes expressing both apology and embarrassment. Perceptively he grasped her feelings and the trace of a smile touched the hard outline of his mouth. He stooped a little, caught her up in his arms, and put her into the car.

'You worry too much,' was his unexpected comment when presently he was sitting beside her. 'When accidents happen we're often thrown into situations which can be a little uncomfortable, but in your case the thing to remember is that you are safe and well—other than that ankle, of course—so just relax, forget any embarrassment you might have felt.'

'You're very kind,' she found herself saying. 'And you're understanding too.'

'Kind? Understanding?' There was no mistaking the undertone of sardonic amusement in his voice. 'You wouldn't have reached a conclusion like that if you knew me a little better, Miss Ridgeway.'

As there was nothing she could find to say to this she merely leant back comfortably as the car rolled smoothly along the drive, its windows open to let in the heady perfumes of the garden. The sun was going down behind a line of grassy kopjes and, spellbound, Lena watched the ever-changing colour against the dark screen of the mountains. Already the silent landscape had been transformed from crimson to gold and now as the gold gave way to the dappled shades of twilight the bushveld became a dark impregnable wilderness, shrouded in mystery and indescribably lonely. Kane stopped the car at the end of the drive before turning on to the slightly wider road that led—over a series of dusty potholes—to Mtula Farm. As usual, a sundown breeze had set in from the mountains and as it murmured through the foliage of the trees it filled the clear air with a tenuous, eerie sort of music. Lena heard it, opened her mouth to remark on it, but then, noting the rigid profile of her companion as he started the car again, she kept her fanciful thoughts to herself, convinced that he would ridicule them—if not verbally then mentally.

The bumpy journey took about ten minutes, as Kane drove very gingerly, taking care of his car, which was long and low and practically new.

'I feel that I've put you to a lot of trouble,' she was saying as he brought the car to a halt outside the front door of Mtula Farm. 'I'm so very sorry.'

'Think no more about it.' He pipped the horn before getting out. The door opened and June stood there, any surprise she evinced being hidden by the swiftly falling shades of night.

'I want to thank you again,' began Lena, but was immediately interrupted as Kane said frowningly, and with undisguised impatience,

'It's not necessary.' He was already assisting her from the car, but—obviously considering her feelings now that another person was present—he wasn't intending to carry her, and for this she sent him a grateful glance, to which there was no response from his rather arrogant countenance. His hands were under her armpits and soon June was exclaiming, asking questions. Kane answered before Lena had the chance of doing so and within a couple of minutes June had been put totally in the picture.

Ten minutes later Kane, having accepted June's invitation to come into the house, but having declined Gerald's offer of a drink, left the house.

Much later, after having been helped to her room by Gerald, Lena stood by the window, her gaze directed to where the homestead lights of Koranna Lodge flickered in the enclosing darkness. A strange and indefinable stirring of her senses had occurred at some profound moment between her meeting with Kane

Westbrook and their bidding each other goodnight. Unable to pick out anything definite, Lena turned impatiently and hopped over to the bed.

'A man with his magnetic personality is bound to have an effect on anyone who meets him for the first time,' she murmured to herself as she settled down beneath the covers. 'In any case, it *was* rather embarrassing, having him lift me in and out of the bath. I except that's the reason why I can't get him out of my thoughts.' And, satisfied with this conclusion, Lena turned on her side and almost immediately succumbed to the call of sleep.

CHAPTER THREE

'It looks as if your ankle is going to be right for the barbecue.' June spoke as she and Lena sat on the shady back stoep, having an afternoon cup of tea. Gerald was in Fonteinville, having gone to collect a farm implement that had been repaired and also to pick up the mail. Lena had asked him to order her a book and it was only after she had gone that the thought occurred to her that she might have left here before the book arrived, since she surmised it would have to come from England. 'It seems to be much better.'

'At least I can hobble about on it now. At first it was so painful that I couldn't bear to put it on the ground.' Recollection brought the inevitable flush to her cheeks and June laughed.

'I'd have given anything to have witnessed the aloof and unemotional Kane Westbrook putting you into the bath!'

Lena's colour deepened. She reached for her cup and took a drink.

'It was embarrassing, I can assure you. But I did have the towel wrapped all around me, as I told you.'

June laughed again.

'I wonder what his thoughts were? You know, he's had a few affairs in his time. He's having one now, as a matter of fact.'

'He is?' Lena glanced swiftly at her across the table, aware of a sudden curiosity to know more about Kane's affair. This curiosity puzzled her, since she was not in the least interested in the amorous activities of Kane Westbrook. All the interest she had in him constituted gratitude for what he had done for her.

Looking back now she had no doubts at all that he

had saved her life, since, once she had been carried from that bank into deeper waters that were increasing both in volume and velocity, there would have been no chance at all of her escaping the fate of drowning. Lena would have wished to thank him again, when she and he met at the barbecue, but, convinced that nothing would annoy him more than a reintroduction of the incident, she resigned herself to the idea of not mentioning it again—ever. Thinking about her experience now, she gave a shudder and her friend said quickly,

'Don't think about what might have happened, Lena. Just let the whole thing be remembered as a lesson.'

'It'll certainly be that,' returned Lena feelingly. 'I'll never again so much as step off the bank.'

'Oh, I don't know. Kane has a boat which, at certain times of the year when the Klein Umgola is carrying sufficient water but isn't a torrent, he sails. We've been on it a couple of times and I assure you it was fun. He might ask us all again and if he does he'll be bound to invite you as well.'

Allowing this to pass without comment, Lena reverted to the subject of Kane's girl-friend.

'You were saying that he's having an affair . . .?'

'Yes. A Mr Davenham came over from England a year ago and began farming. About a couple of months ago his niece, Magda, arrived and decided to stay. She has no parents and as she was living quite alone she saw no reason for going back—especially as she had met the devastatingly attractive Kane Westbrook, and fallen for him like a ton of bricks.'

'She had?' Lena's eyes were pensively fixed on the two boys working together in the mealies. In the far distance, conical-shaped against the clear limpid sky, could be discerned the native village in which they lived, with their wives and piccanins. 'What's she like?'

'Beautiful, in the ash-blonde, peach-bloom skin sort of way. She's supposed to be working for—or with—her uncle, but each time I've seen her she's looked as if she had just got herself ready to attend a wedding!'

Instinctively Lena glanced down at her hands; already they were giving evidence of her interest in the garden.

'She doesn't sound cut out for work on a farm,' she said at length. And June immediately shook her head, a gesture of agreement.

'More cut out to lead the lady's life, I should say.'

'Where did she and Kane meet?' Again Lena was asking herself the reason for her curiosity. It was totally out of character, as anyone who knew her would without hesitation have declared.

'At the Impala Club in Fonteinville. You'll be going there quite soon.'

'I will?'

June nodded.

'They have dinner-dances once a month. If your ankle's all right we shall book for a fortnight tonight. Everyone goes, and it'll be nice for you that you've already met some of them at Kane's barbecue.'

'Do you dress up?'

'Of course—it's an excuse to don all your finery, and your jewels,' added June with a laugh.

Lena thought of this girl, Magda, and wondered what sort of 'finery' she possessed.

June was frowning in thought and suddenly she said,

'You know, Lena, it's just dawned on me that this affair with Magda might be serious. After all, Koranna Lodge does need a mistress, and who better than Magda? She's both intelligent and decorative—all

Kane would want in a wife.'

'All?' in some considerable surprise. 'A man usually desires much more than those things.'

'Not Kane,' with firm conviction. 'He and Magda are very suited, simply because they're so much alike.' Picking up her cup, June took a drink, her eyes wandering to the row of dome palms which had suddenly begun swaying as the breeze freshened. It was going to rain, decided Lena, following the direction of her gaze and murmuring, in response to what June had said,

'They are?'

'Undoubtedly. You've met Kane, so you know how totally unemotional he is. Well, Magda's as cold as charity, too. Yes . . . come to think of it, Kane could very well be serious with her. She's got what it takes in looks—with that glorious hair and delicate skin and eyes that know what they're there for.'

'Eyes that...?' Lena threw her an interrogating glance and, laughing, June said humorously,

'She can use them most effectively when there are men around—— But why should I try to explain? You'll realize what I mean when you see her antics at the barbecue!'

'You don't appear to like her very much.' Lena was frowning inwardly; she could not have said why, but the idea of Kane's marrying someone who was of an unattractive disposition was more than a little disturbing to her.

'Frankly, I don't—but it could be envy,' confessed June, a humorous gleam in her eyes. A short while later she went off to do some household chores, flatly refusing to allow Lena to help her. She must rest that ankle, she ordered in her usual forceful manner. But, once she had gone, Lena proceeded to the garden to finish some weeding she had begun that morning, a task that had proved to be comparatively easy, since

Lena could do it on her knees.

The evening of the barbecue arrived and although her ankle was still bandaged for support, it was not giving Lena any pain, and therefore she was no longer walking with a pronounced limp.

'What are you wearing?' June asked the question just as Lena was going up to her room to wash and change. 'These events are informal, yet you don't feel you've done wrong if you decide to dress up. I've been to a barbecue in a long dress, but I've also been to one in jeans.'

'I look such a scrag in jeans these days.'

'You're filling out—gradually,' laughed June, her green eyes roving Lena's figure. 'My cooking, of course!'

'It is, too,' returned Lena sincerely. 'Sometimes I can't believe my good fortune in coming here and living like a lady of leisure.'

'Come off it! Don't you deceive yourself that I haven't been observing you, buzzing off quietly and getting on with your gardening!'

Lena laughed then and said,

'I love it! It's so easy to grow things——'

'Not for me. I always forget to water the darned plants.'

'I've ordered some roses from Fonteinville.' Lena paused, looking a trifle doubtfully at her friend. 'You don't mind my putting things in?'

'I'm delighted. I'd love to have a garden that looked something like Kane's.'

'From what little I saw it would appear that he's spent a great deal of money on his gardens?'

June nodded, but went on to say that many of the flowering trees and shrubs had been put there by his grandfather.

'He was lucky, inheriting that gorgeous place, and

it'll be a lucky girl who becomes mistress of it—if ever a girl does become mistress of it, that is.'

While they were talking Lena had been making a cursory examination of the clothes in her wardrobe. She took out a long dress in brushed nylon but, shaking her head, returned it to the rail.

'I think I'll wear jeans and a shirt, after all,' she said.

'I'm wearing my new trouser suit. It's thin, and sort of eveningy without being formal.'

Lena wished she had something like that; however, she did have a pair of well-cut white jeans and with those she wore a coral-coloured sweater with a high, roll-over collar. Her hair, newly washed, and fast becoming more healthy, shone when she brushed it, and her eyes shone also. But her face was still thin, and her cheeks pale. She applied the blusher, and a little colour to her lips, eventually satisfying herself that she had done just about all she could in the way of making herself look attractive. Subconsciously, she had wished all along to make a good impression on the people she would meet at the barbecue. Once, she had been a popular member of the club in her town; her friends had been many. But soon after her father's marriage she had found herself with so many chores to do when she came home from the office in the evenings that her social life had practically ceased even before the tragic deaths of her father and stepmother had resulted in the total responsibility of the children being thrust upon her.

Twilight came down soon after Gerald and June and Lena arrived at Koranna Lodge. Kane, incredibly tall and arresting in a white tropical suit which contrasted most attractively with the tawny bronze of his face and hands, was there to greet them. His eyes rested for a moment on Lena's face; she could not help flushing as she remembered with painful clarity his putting her into the bath and taking her out after she had bathed and rinsed her hair. Was he amused? His lips seemed to twitch slightly, but there was no reflection of humour in the hard stare he gave her. His greeting, too, was crisp. However, this meeting was as her first meeting with him should have been—free from annoyance on his part and from embarrassment on hers.

'How's the ankle?' he asked with the politeness which as a gentleman he should exhibit, but he was distant for all that.

'Much better, thank you, Mr Westbrook. I didn't consult a doctor.'

He merely nodded his head, then turned to say something to Gerald about a couple of heifers which Gerald had bought from a man recommended by Kane.

More guests arrived; Kane greeted them courteously enough, but very noticeable indeed was that aloofness mentioned by June and which Lena herself had observed. Yet, standing some way away after she had been introduced to these new arrivals, Lena was rather surprised to discover that Kane was not averse to chatting with his guests if they themselves were that way inclined.

'He's not spontaneously hail-fellow-well-met,' laughed June when Lena remarked on her observations, 'but he has a way of setting everyone totally at his or her ease and then displaying that requisite degree of politeness which makes the perfect host. You'll enjoy yourself tonight—and so will everyone else. Kane's barbecues and dinner-parties are always something to look forward to, and I know of no one who, having been sent an invitation, wouldn't be disappointed should anything occur that prevented them from attending.'

'He's decidedly attractive,' mused Lena, her eyes still fixed on his face. Illumination had been arranged in the trees, illumination of many colours; he stood beneath the long line of yellow lights which had been fitted among the passion vines shading the terrace, and every classical line of his impressive features was revealed. The low forehead, the cheekbones prominent and high, which created the impression of angularity; the hollows below them, the strongly defined jawline and firm chin ... Lena's eyes moved to his grey ones, noting the dark, metallic light in them. His hair, waving and long enough to cover his ears, was light brown ... and for no reason at all Lena's mind gave forth a picture of the man she had imagined marrying. Tall and dark and handsome. Dark ... she liked jet black hair best of all in a man; it had character and strength. And yet, as she looked at Kane's hair, shining beneath the lights, she decided she would never see a man with hair more attractive than his.

What musings! She cast them off and when June suggested they wander around the grounds Lena was only to eager to agree. That man was altogether too magnetic; he could draw without even knowing that he did it.

The moon was full, yellow and incredibly large. It shone down on the garden which Lena saw, even by this limited illumination, was a veritable paradise of beauty. Down through the years nothing had been spared by way of expense. Hibiscus abounded, and allamandas with their glossy green leaves forming an enchanting framework for the velvety golden bells which Lena had heard described as 'solified sunshine'. Poincianas whose scarlet long-clawed petal blossoms measured three or four inches across and at a certain stage of their growth resembled orchids; frangipani whose enchantment included fragrance as well as the sheer beauty of its waxy white and crimson blossoms. Passion flowers and anthuriums, the sweet aloes and bird of paradise.

Lena's appreciative eyes shone with the wonderment of it all. She felt that nowhere could there be a garden to excel this.

'I'm breathless with it all!' she exclaimed when at length they were wandering back towards the lights and the chatter of people. Gentle unobtrusive strains of music came from some obscure place to mingle with the sound of cicadas' wings rubbing together in the darkness. 'Kane must be exceedingly proud of his home.'

'He's a proud man altogether. I suppose he has a right to be, owning a mansion like this, set in such incredibly beautiful grounds. I love coming here, as you can well imagine.'

Lena nodded her head, her eye catching Kane's tall figure as he moved among his guests. He strode towards the two girls, smiled faintly as he invited them to take drinks on the terrace.

'I've been showing Lena round your gardens, Kane. She's thrilled with them—as I am myself.'

His eyes flickered from June to Lena, remaining impassively on her face.

'You obviously appreciate the beauty of flowers, Miss Ridgeway,' he commented suavely. 'You must come in the daytime. We'll fix something later. Meanwhile, you'll have to excuse me; I see another couple of guests have arrived.'

He went away, but five minutes later he had joined them on the terrace. Gerald was with them and the four sat and chatted for some time before Kane said,

'The food's ready, I believe. Do help yourselves.' He and Gerald strolled away together; June and Lena followed slowly and eventually the two men were no longer to be seen.

'This girl—Magda,' ventured Lena at length, hoping that June would not notice her interest in Kane's friend, 'she isn't here, apparently.'

'She'll come. Magda's one of those people who deliberately arrive late so as to make an "entrance", but what she seems to have forgotten this time is that at a barbecue people tend not to notice new arrivals simply because everyone's mingling with everyone else, and secondly, because the light isn't all that good. My, but there's a nice large crowd here tonight!' she went on, changing the subject. 'Before we eat I'll introduce you to Phil and Janey Thorsby; they keep the general store in town. And there's the president of the Yacht Club and his wife. They're great people!'

As Mr and Mrs Burnett were already approaching the spot where the girls stood, by a hedge of perfumed acacias, June introduced them and the four stood chatting for a while under the trees.

'So you're on holiday here?' Mrs Burnett, tall and distinguished-looking with her firm features and iron-grey hair, smiled at Lena in the most friendly way. 'And how do you like our country?'

'It's beautiful,' was Lena's enthusiastic rejoinder, 'what bit I've seen of it, that is.'

'Lena's crazy about flowers,' put in June. 'She's going to transform our sorry little plot to something rather grand.'

'No,' exclaimed Lena with a slight rise of colour to her cheeks. 'I'm merely pottering, Mrs Burnett. Take no notice of what June says.'

'Well,' interposed Mr Burnett, 'you should get plenty of ideas here——' He swept a hand, embracing the immediate scene of trees and shrubs and the medley of exotic plants whose perfume filled the still, crystal air. 'I'm afraid many of us have pinched ideas from this incredibly lovely place.' He stopped as one of Kane's dusky houseboys appeared beside him with a tray of sparkling glasses.

'You like a drink, baas?' he asked, at which Mr Burnett flicked a finger, indicating that he should ask the ladies first. 'Yes, baas,' grinned the boy, obeying the unspoken command and serving Mrs Burnett and the two girls before returning to Mr Burnett.

'What a pleasant occasion.' Mr Burnett glanced around, glass in hand. 'How is it that Kane always makes such a roaring success of everything he does?'

'Because he's efficient, darling,' from his wife, with a smile. 'His plans are always made with such meticulous care.'

'A paragon of all the virtues as well as being easy on the eyes!' whispered June with a grin when both Mr and Mrs Burnett turned to acknowledge a greeting from two members of the Yacht Club.

'You must bring Lena along to our next dance,' smiled Mr Burnett when presently he and his wife were preparing to stroll away towards some friends who were obviously waiting for them. 'I'll see that you receive a written invitation.'

'Thank you,' returned Lena. 'You're very kind.'

'Not at all. We like to make visitors welcome—so that they'll come again,' he added with a benign little twinkle to his eye. 'You see, we rather welcome having people come to visit us.'

Phil and Janey proved to be equally charming, although much younger than the Burnetts. Janey, dark and rather plump, was a Scot, having met Phil when he was at the university in Edinburgh. She and he had been married for almost five years and for four of those they had kept the shop, having decided to leave their farm—which was small and, therefore, not profitable to run—and take over the shop from the people who were retiring.

'Come in when you're in town,' Janey invited Lena eagerly. 'You don't have to buy anything; just pop in for a chat!'

'What friendly people,' Lena was saying when at last she and June were making for the place where the food was being prepared, by Kane's houseboys and other servants. 'I shan't want to leave; that's for sure!'

'You won't?'

The two girls turned—to look up into the bronzed unsmiling face of their host.

'Lena's charmed with our country,' laughed June. 'I think we shall have to find her a husband, don't you, Kane?' The three were strolling along together now. Kane glanced down into Lena's face.

'There aren't many unattached men around here, I'm afraid,' he said.

'What about Rex Lloyd—and his brother, for that matter?'

'Stephen? He's at least thirty-five. Far too old for Miss Ridgeway.'

Lena lowered her eyes. Kane was thirty-five ... she was thinking that this was a most attractive age indeed for a man. With Kane—well, he possessed all the maturity that made for wisdom and efficiency, while at the same time being young enough to enjoy life to the full.

'I wouldn't call thirty-five old,' returned June.

'I didn't say it was. I did say that Stephen was too old for Miss Ridgeway.'

How old, wondered Lena, was Magda?

'What about Rex, then?' from June roguishly. But Lena, becoming embarrassed by what to June was obviously fun, broke in to say,

'I'm not looking for a husband, June. I like my single state.' Which was quite true, of course. Not that she imagined remaining single all her life. One day, perhaps in the far distant future, her ideal would come along and, if he happened to be as attractive to her as he was to him, then she would marry. Now, however, she was thoroughly enjoying the life that had been made possible through the generosity of June and Gerald, and had no intention of becoming involved in anything which could disturb this most peaceful and pleasant existence.

'Every single woman is looking for a husband.' This, spoken in tones of sardonic conviction, came from Kane, and Lena glanced swiftly up at him, her colour fluctuating. A retort left her lips before she could prevent it.

'No such thing, Mr Westbrook! How have you reached a conclusion like that?' Her rush of anger, although not particularly emphasized, was plainly evident, and it surprised him.

'You're certainly touchy about it,' he remarked.

Feeling that it was time she intervened, June laughingly declared that she was hungry and pleaded that—if they must begin an argument—it should be left in obeyance for the time being. At which Kane responded to her laugh and, taking the arms of both girls, he steered them across the wide velvet lawn to where, under a canopy of yellowwoods, the cooking-stoves were glowing red.

People stood around, plates in hand, chatting and laughing while they waited to be served with sizzling cutlets or crisp brown portions of chicken. On nearby tables were to be found all the necessary garnishings, and numerous cold dishes besides.

Having seen that the two girls had all they required, and having found them a vacant table under a mango tree from whose branches hung several red and yellow lanterns, Kane said with his customary conventional politeness,

'I'm sorry to leave you, but I see that another guest has arrived,' and he gave a slight inclination of his shoulders before moving away, Lena's brown eyes following his tall figure as it took the direction that brought him up to the girl who had just arrived.

'Magda,' said June unnecessarily. It couldn't be anyone else, thought Lena, noting the ash-blonde hair, gleaming in the moonlight. 'Just take an eyeful of what she's got on!'

A slinky black trouser suit made from material in which numerous silver threads glinted. Collar, cuffs and pockets glittered even brighter, trimmed as they were with sequins. The girl's hair was immaculately coiffured, drawn back tightly with a plait going over the top of her head.

'She looks most attractive,' Lena had to admit. 'Her outfit must have cost a fortune.'

June nodded, saying that Magda had recently spent a few days in Johannesburg and, therefore, had probably bought the trouser suit there.

'It isn't the thing for a barbecue, though,' added June with a hint of spite not unmingled with envy. 'It's more suitable for the events that go on at the Club.'

'I'm very much looking forward to going to the Club.'

'You certainly get to know people. There's a small town community, and they started the Club originally, as a means of social fusing, as it were. However, all the far-flung farmers and timber growers began attending the functions, and now we're all members.'

'Shall I have to become a member?'

'It would be a good idea, if you're staying any length of time. Meanwhile, you can be our guest.'

'The Yacht Club,' murmured Lena, her eyes wandering again to the couple who, having greeted each other with smiles, were now strolling towards the table at which Lena and June were sitting, 'where is it?'

'On a very wide part of the river, about five miles west of the town.'

'Does Kane have a yacht?'

'Not now. He used to own one, though.'

Lena tried to imagine him in nautical clothes, sailing a graceful vessel along the river. It was not difficult to bring such a picture into focus.

'Kane's coming over ...'

'You're in for the doubtful pleasure of meeting his girl-friend.'

'Hello, June.' Magda's effusive greeting came forth at the same time as Kane's.

'Miss Ridgeway, may I introduce you to Magda Sanborn—a friend of mine whose uncle runs Wisel Farm, which is located on the other side of Fonteinville.'

'How do you do?' Lena glanced up at the girl, admitting to her glowing perfection. Magda looked down indifferently as she responded to Lena's softly-spoken words.

'Miss Ridgeway's staying with June and Gerald for a while,' explained Kane.

'You're on holiday?' A perfunctory smile accompanied Magda's question. 'How long for?'

'I don't know. I haven't any ties in England, so I can stay as long as I like.' Not without working, though, thought Lena. A few weeks was all right, but should she want to stay on then she would have to begin contributing something to the grocery bill.

'You're very fortunate.' The girl's manner, though pleasant enough, was somehow lacking in sincerity. Lena gained the impression that she had been branded colourless by the golden girl who, with a sudden possessive movement, had slipped her arm through Kane's. 'I hope you enjoy your stay,' Magda thought to add before she and Kane moved away, to stand chatting with Mr and Mrs Burnett who were over by the table on which was spread an exciting array of sweets and pastries made by Kane's most excellent cook, an African who had learned his trade from a London-trained cook who had worked for Kane several years previously. Joseph had almost from the first excelled his predecessor.

Lena watched, then the couple moved away; the next time she caught sight of them they were disappearing into the darkness of the wooded enclosure on the far side of the grounds . . .

'Ah, here's the young man I was talking about!' June's cheerful exclamation brought Lena's eyes back from the place where she had last seen Kane and his girl-friend. 'Rex Lloyd.'

Coming up to the table, the young man smilingly asked if he could join them.

'But of course.' June's ready permission being followed by the introduction, Lena found herself being subjected to a stare of rather keen interest as Rex Lloyd took possession of the vacant chair. A citrus grower, he lived at Dakana Farm with his brother and sister. Both were on a visit to friends at present, Rex explained, and so he was on his own this evening.

'Well, you can have company now,' from June with a smile. 'Lena's willing to keep you company, aren't you?'

Lena said yes—simply because she could scarcely say no.

However, as Rex was not in any way unattractive it was no hardship to have his company, she thought when, later, she and he were walking in the grounds. Dark-haired and handsome in a rugged sort of way, he made no attempt to conceal the fact that Lena appealed to him.

'It's good to know you're staying for a while, Lena.' His voice was eager as he went on to invite her over to Dakana Farm. 'We're having a small dinner party for my sister's birthday; it's on Wednesday week. You'll come?'

She hesitated, but not for long.

'Yes, I'd love to—and thank you very much for asking me,' she returned with a smile. However, as time passed and it looked as if he intended to monopolize her she made an excuse and went over to rejoin June and Gerald. Within seconds Kane came to join them.

'You're enjoying yourself?' he inquired of Lena politely.

'Very much, thank you, Mr Westbrook.' She was shy all at once, and he seemed to know it, for a shaft of a smile touched his lips.

'And you, June?' he said, his glance including her husband.

'Of course—as always,' returned June. 'How do you do it, Kane? If we gave a barbecue it wouldn't be a success like this!'

'Nonsense! If your dinner-party the other week was anything to go by you'd certainly make a success of a barbecue.'

Lena looked up at him with her big expressive eyes. Here was a side to him that was definitely attractive.

'You're being kind, but——'

'No such thing, June.' He turned to Gerald. 'You shouldn't allow her to talk like that,' he said. 'June is an excellent hostess.'

'Allow!' June seized on that, as Lena had suspected she would—although she had not thought that she would actually voice her complaint of its use. 'What an old-fashioned word to use in that particular context, Kane. You sound like an autocratic Victorian husband!'

He laughed—and Lena caught her breath. The man's attractions were becoming more noticeably apparent to her. It seemed difficult that on first having him described to her by June, she had decided that his character was far from pleasant. His eyes were also laughing as they moved to Lena's upturned face, their attention caught because of her fixed unblinking stare. She flushed and glanced away, recalling the revelation that had come to her on the evening of the day he had rescued her from the river. She had known that at some unremembered moment, a strange stirring of her senses had occurred. She now felt a similar sensation—but this time she would be able to recall it without the least difficulty.

'Autocratic?' he repeated at last, pausing to consider the word. 'Are you really serious?' he asked, surprising them all.

'Of course!' June looked saucily at him. 'Why the pained expression?' she went on intrepidly. 'You must know your own character!'

'June,' protested Gerald, 'you're going beyond the boundary of politeness!'

'Am I?' The question was addressed to Kane. Glancing at Gerald, Lena saw at once that he was uncomfortable, although she could not see why he should be, for June wasn't being rude to her host. Gerald ought to know his wife's ways by now, she thought.

'No,' answered Kane, but with a sort of studied politeness which was difficult to interpret.

'June,' interposed Gerald, glancing round. 'I believe Mary and James Brownlow are wanting us.'

'Oh...' June turned her head. 'They are?' She looked up at Kane. 'Would you excuse us?'

He nodded, his eyes following the couple as they

strolled away, and then he turned to Lena.

'How about something to eat?' he suggested. 'Or have you had all you want?'

'No—I do feel a bit hungry.' Awkwardness swept over her at being alone with him. 'I did have something earlier, as you know, but——'

'Come along, then,' he broke in, as if he sensed her awkwardness and wished to dispel it. 'We'll find a place to sit—over there, under the trees.' She trotted to keep pace with him as he strode towards the cooking-stoves. Dark-skinned women served Lena with sausages and mushrooms, while Kane had a couple of chicken legs. They sat under the trees, their plates on their knees. Lights and music and perfumes gave the whole scene a romantic quality. Lena looked at her companion's aristocratic profile and wondered if he were thinking of Magda.

'As I was saying, you must come over during the daytime.' Kane turned his head as he spoke; she saw the hint of a smile that touched his lips. 'How about tomorrow afternoon?'

'That'll be lovely!' The sudden eagerness in her voice was reflected in her eyes and she saw again that he was regarding her with interest. 'Thank you very much for asking me.'

'It's always a pleasure to me when someone shows appreciation of the gardens of Koranna Lodge. I myself can claim very little credit for what they are today. My grandfather was an enthusiast where flowers were concerned; he intended that these grounds should become a showpiece.'

'He succeeded,' she returned without hesitation. 'I think he must have been a—a . . .' She let her voice trail away to silence, and Kane, perceptively guessing why, was urged to prompt her.

'Yes?'

'Oh—er—nothing.' She coloured, and secretly hoped that the shadows caused by the foliage of the trees would overset the lights that twinkled among the branches. She had no wish that he should note her rising colour.

'I believe that you were going to voice the opinion that my grandfather was an extraordinary person.'

She nodded her head.

'Yes, I was.'

'Then why did you hesitate?'

'It seemed an impertinence to voice that opinion. After all, I'm a stranger to you.'

'A stranger?' with a quizzical lift of his brows. 'Not quite, I think.'

She swallowed, her feelings very mixed indeed. Overawed by his powerful personality and general air of superiority, she felt she would have welcomed an intrusion by one or other of the guests. And yet, on the other hand, she had a subconscious desire to be alone with him, to have his entire attention to herself. Deciding that the ideal would be for her to feel totally at her ease with him, she endeavoured to inject some measure of confidence into her voice when next she spoke, changing the subject as she referred to her projected visit of the following afternoon.

'What time would you like me to come tomorrow, Mr Westbrook?'

'I shall be free to show you around any time after three. Until then I shall be busy supervising some land-clearing I'm having done.'

'I'll come along at about half-past three, then?'

'Fine.' A silence followed; Lena felt an unaccountable prickling of her spine and instinctively turned her head, peering into the darkness of the woods behind her. All was silent except for the cicadas—and the soft strains of the music coming from the direction of the house.

'Is—is anyone there?' she whispered nervously. 'I know it's silly, but I sensed the presence of someone, in the woods behind us.'

Kane merely laughed and assured her that no one would be hiding in the woods.

Much later Lena was alone admiring a bed of canna flowers, when, without warning, Magda came up beside her. Lena jumped, a spark of anger showing in her eyes because of the furtive manner of the girl's approach. 'She must have known it would startle me,' whispered Lena to herself.

'Do you mind if I join you?' asked Magda pleasantly. 'Kane's such a stickler for etiquette and all the other niceties which characterize the perfect host that I find myself alone on occasions. I thought it would be pleasant to get to know you.'

Again Lena sensed the insincerity, but she could not put that forward as an excuse for snubbing the girl. And so she gave her a smile and said,

'Shall we sit down, then—over there, by the fountain?'

'That would be nice.' Magda led the way, just as if she were the hostess caring for the comfort of one of her guests, thought Lena, who followed, wondering what she and Magda would find to talk about. 'What made you decide to come over to South Africa for a holiday?' asked Magda without preamble. 'I mean—the fare's quite costly.'

'My friends were over in England, visiting relatives. I decided to come back with them.'

'And you don't know how long you're staying?'

'I have no idea how long I'm staying.' Lena hoped the coolness in her voice was escaping Magda, though she rather thought the girl must have noticed it, since it was so pronounced.

'I—er—have heard that you're coming over here—to Koranna Lodge—tomorrow afternoon?'

Lena's senses became alert. She inquired curiously,

'How do you know? Did Mr Westbrook tell you?'

The girl hesitated, seeming to have difficulty in finding suitable words.

'N-no...' Another pause. 'I happened to overhear you and him talking.'

Lena's eyes wandered over to the north edge of the garden, to where she and Kane were sitting at the time she had sensed a presence in the woods behind her.

'When we were over on that seat?' She gestured with her hand. 'You were in the woods?' She turned, so that she could see the girl full-face, but Magda also turned her head and Lena was left looking at her profile.

'Yes,' admitted the girl at last. 'I was strolling by at the time.'

'By ... or in the woods?'

At the tone in Lena's voice the girl turned sharply and snapped,

'That note of contempt in your voice, Miss Ridgeway! What exactly does it mean?'

Pausing in indecision, Lena at last replied,

'I had an idea that someone was in the woods behind us——'

'You're insinuating that I was listening to you and Kane! Oh, how dare you! I shall complain to him——'

'Miss Sanborn,' broke in Lena with some asperity, 'you're jumping to conclusions. I didn't insinuate anything!'

What a situation! Here she was, almost quarrelling with a girl who was a stranger to her!

'Yes, you did! I'm absolutely sure of it!'

Lena gave an impatient sigh.

'In that case, Miss Sanborn, there's nothing I can do to disabuse you, is there?'

Silence. Magda had assumed an injured expression and with a shrug Lena rose to her feet and walked away, no doubt at all in her mind that Magda had deliberately eavesdropped, standing there in the darkness of the woods and listening to the conversation going on between Kane Westbrook and herself.

CHAPTER FOUR

THERE was no doubt, thought Lena, that Kane's garden was a kaleidoscope of colour, aflame as it was with tropical splendour. Having met her as she came along his drive, he had spent over an hour showing her around the grounds. Five minutes ago one of his houseboys had come to tell him that he had a visitor, and with a polite word of excuse and apology he had left her to wander alone until his return. She stood, in rapt meditation, wondering what the land was like when, after clearing the bush, Kane's grandfather had begun his programme of planting. She glanced up at the magnificent oak trees, their branches soaring in luxuriant height against the clear brittle sky. Dome palms waved their spidery plumes, stirred by the lazy air currents travelling in from the south-east; mahogany trees, cypresses, cedars and eucalyptus ... so many mature trees to form backcloths for the more ornamental kind—the flamboyants and poinsettias, the South African tulip trees, the frangipanis and bougainvillaeas. Her wandering gaze found beds of golden irises which were interspersed with beds of allamandas and canna flowers; it moved to the fountain, which sprayed into an ornamental pond on which grew the giant African water lilies.

Yes, she mused, this was a paradise in miniature, created because of a man's will to produce something of sheer undiluted beauty. She looked across to where the windmills, silhouetted against the sky, turned in the breeze. Artesian water, Lena had soon learned, was one of South Africa's greatest blessings. No matter how dry the veld, or how long a drought might continue, there was always an abundance of water underneath the ground; in consequence there were always windmills on the skyline; erected by farmers over boreholes, they provided all the water that was required. Many dorps depended entirely on artesian water, Gerald had once told Lena.

'At a few feet down you can get water—brackish, it's true, but water for all that,' Gerald had said when on one occasion Lena had been asking about the problem of water in this hot and arid country. 'Drill to a hundred feet or more and you can be fairly sure of clear water.'

'I'm sorry I had to leave you.' Lena twisted her head as Kane returned. 'It was just a little business I had to attend to.'

'That's all right,' she smiled. 'I've been enjoying every single moment of it.'

'I'm relieved,' he said with that familiar edge of cool politeness to his voice. 'Well, I believe you've seen just about everything. Do you have time to come into the house for some refreshment?'

She nodded, although hesitantly, for it seemed wrong, somehow, to show too much eagerness.

'Thank you very much.'

They strolled back to the house, traversing gravel paths bordered by flowering shrubs in which insects murmured. A black and gold butterfly moth fluttered in front of Lena, so close that she could have reached out a hand and caught it; a couple of redwings swooped, then rose again into the perfume-laden air, and disappeared among the trees. The velvet lawn spread away towards the house; Kane and Lena crossed it, passing massive specimen trees standing in splendid isolation, bright-plumaged birds chittering in their branches, exotic flowers blooming at the bases of their trunks.

'We'll have our refreshments on the stoep; it's always cooler there.' Lena nodded in agreement. After the bright flood of noonday sunshine, when the veld had shimmered under its brittle heat, the afternoon had become close and oppressive, but now a faint breeze drifted in from the mountains to cool the stoep which had already been protected from the sun's rays by the trellised vines that had been trained up its sides and which completely covered its roof. 'What would you like to drink?' Having brought out a chair for her, Kane stood aside while she took possession of it.

'Something cool, please—an iced lemonade or something similar.' She was awkward again and it vexed her, for during the past hour or so she had managed very well to carry on a conversation with him, never once feeling overpowered either by his magnetic personality or by his cool impersonal manner of speech.

He went away; she twisted her head to watch his incredibly tall straight figure as he stepped from the stoep into the room beyond. What a pleasant afternoon it had been, strolling about the beautiful grounds of Koranna Lodge ... with its handsome aristocratic owner. Contentment had been Lena's predominant motif, her senses responding to the solitude and static silence of the limitless bushveld, her nostrils filled with the admixture of flower perfumes and the pungent, resinous smell of the Aleppo pines growing in the vast forest owned by Kane. She looked down the valley, aware that he possessed every inch of it. To the north of the valley was the impressive majesty of the mountains, to the west and south the lush green of the farmlands and to the east the line of kopjes, dark and gaunt against the sky.

Kane returned and a smile fluttered to Lena's lips. Kane stood for a moment, his grey metallic eyes inscrutable. No smile rose to his mouth in response to hers. How unapproachable he was!

'Liesel will be out with the drinks directly,' he told her in that cool impersonal tone to which she had become used. 'We'll not waste too much time over our drinks as it's going to rain. I'd better take you home in the car.' He was glancing at the sky as he spoke. Lena herself had been in Africa long enough to be able to read the signs. The rain of which he spoke would in all probability be accompanied by thunder and lightning.

Liesel appeared, a slender, doe-eyed native girl with a hesitant smile. She said in excellent English,

'Your drinks, Mr Westbrook.'

'Thank you.' The gracious edge to his tone was pronounced; it brought response in the deepening of the girl's smile. Putting down the iced fruit drinks, which were served in hand-engraved lead-crystal tumblers, she went away.

'Are you seriously wanting to transform Gerald's garden?' inquired Kane after a small silence. 'If so, I must let you have some plants and cuttings. Let me know what you would like.'

Lena glanced swiftly at him, astounded at the offer.

'That's most kind of you. I am trying to improve the garden, and June's given me a free hand, but I'm not an expert and I wouldn't know what would grow in that particular type of soil.'

'The soil's exactly like mine. so anything you've seen here will grow at Mtula Farm.' Kane twirled his glass and she heard the ice tinkle against the side. 'The garden at Mtula Farm is rather well placed for improvement, having the terraces and the large flat area that could be made into a level and very attractive lawn.' He became thoughtful, speculatively observing the small vortex he was creating in his glass. 'Yes, the garden there certainly has potential.'

Lena's eyes lighted up; Kane's words were a challenge which fired her with the urge to produce something beautiful out of the present nondescript gardens surrounding the Van de Merwes homestead.

'Would you—advise me about how to begin?' she asked, rather hesitantly because it did dawn on her that her request might not be welcomed by Kane, busy as he always was with the running of his own vast estate. But she need not have worried; he was more than willing to give her all the advice she might ask of him, he informed her graciously. 'Thank you,' she returned with a smile. 'I shall become quite excited about the project.'

Faintly he smiled, his grey eyes holding hers for a while before slowly moving over the rest of her face. She lowered her lashes, uncomfortable under his observation, for she felt sure that, pale and thin as her face was, he must be branding her colourless and unattractive in comparison to the dazzling Magda Sanborn.

'The transformation you're obviously intending to bring about will take some time,' he warned at length. 'You're prepared for that?'

She found herself hesitating, disturbed by the uncertainty of the length of her stay at Mtula Farm.

'How long, Mr Westbrook?' she inquired at last.

'A few months. It's true that here, so long as you are free with your use of water—and fortunately, Gerald has plenty of it—things grow quickly. However, this growth speed doesn't happen to be the chief consideration with a garden that's been neglected. You'll have a great deal of clearing of weeds to do; also there'll be some digging.' He paused, thoughtfully twisting his glass again. 'And if you decide to have a lawn then there'll be both the digging and the levelling—these in addition to the initial clearance of weeds, that is.'

'I see.' Lena frowned in thought. 'I don't know how long I shall be staying, that's the difficulty.'

He seemed surprised by this statement.

'Gerald gave me to understand that your stay would be a prolonged one.'

'Both he and June have said, more than once, that I can stay as long as I like. But——' She stopped for a moment, thinking she had heard the distant sound of thunder. 'I'd like to stay indefinitely,' she added presently, sending him a wry smile, 'but it wouldn't be practicable unless I could get a job.'

'No, I suppose not. However, I take it that your stay will in fact be of sufficient length to enable you to do some work on the garden?' Before she could answer he had added, 'It'll be a pity if you yourself are not going to be able to enjoy the results of all your work.'

'I don't mind that. The actual creation of something beautiful will be reward enough.'

'I like your attitude,' he returned, with such promptitude that it was undoubtedly a sincere compliment, and Lena, her whole mind attuned to the new emotions which had emerged within her, flushed daintily as a surge of sheer pleasure swept through her whole body. What was happening to her? she wondered, staring studiously at her glass, aware that she must avoid the disconcerting gaze of Kane's dark, metallic eyes.

He spoke at length, saying that they had better be on their way.

'We'll discuss your requirements when I come over to Mtula Farm the day after tomorrow,' he went on, adding that he was coming over at the invitation of Gerald, who had asked for some advice on what crops to grow on the two new fields which he had just acquired, fields which had been unused for so long that they had almost reverted back to the original bush. 'Drink up, Miss Ridgeway,' said Kane, looking at her glass. 'We'll have to make haste if we're to miss the storm.'

He went to fetch the car; this being so reminiscent of that other occasion when he had gone to fetch the car in order to take her home it was inevitable that in a flood of memory it should all come back to her—the falling into the water, Kane's strong arms outstretched as he hauled her to safety, his imperious manner when stating that she must have a hot bath. Then all that followed ... his lifting her into the bath, then taking her out again. Looking back now, Lena vividly recalled that feeling of unreality. The same sensation was upon her at this moment, as she waited on the stoep, the air sultry and ominous around her, for the sound of Kane's car, the engine starting, the revving up, the gliding movement before the car crunched to a standstill in front of her. Profoundly conscious of emotions that had already been stirred on two occasions, Lena became tensed as the deep silence of waiting continued. Subconsciously she was aware of a background to the silence—the chittering sound of cicadas in the trees.

Sundown was already advancing as she stepped into the car; soon the brief eastern twilight would enshroud the fields, and add regality to the distant massif, clothing its majestic crags with several shades of purple. Suddenly, just as Kane was about to start the car rolling along the drive, the air became still and a strange, eerie radiance shed its glow over the garden and the house and the farm buildings in the distance. The conical outline of the native village took on the aspect of something of mystic origin. Within seconds a primeval silence hung over the entire landscape. Great black cumulo-nimbus clouds rolled across the sky, and the eerie radiance gave way to a deep, impenetrable gloom. Turning her head, Lena spoke, remarking on the dramatic change in the atmosphere; she felt she ought to have whispered, so profoundly conscious was she of the hush that surrounded her and Kane.

'I'm not sure whether or not to wait——' Kane's voice, edged with uncertainty, was abruptly cut short as a vivid flash of lightning lit the sky, to be followed by a clap of thunder, prelude to the downpour that was to come. 'We'll go back inside,' he said without further hesitation. 'It'll probably not last too long.'

They had just entered the house when the rain came, pouring down like a waterfall.

'It's always so sudden here,' commented Lena when they were in the long, low-windowed living-room. 'You don't get much warning.' She looked at Kane from her comfortable place on the sofa, her limpid eyes shining in a way they had not shone for some considerable time.

'You look happy,' commented Kane unexpectedly as he sat down. 'You're obviously having a most enjoyable time with your friends.'

'It is rather wonderful,' she agreed enthusiastically. 'Life's suddenly become an exciting experience.'

Kane's eyes opened wide at the manner of her phrasing.

'Because of your appreciation of the miracle of nature, I think?' Grave his tones; with a flash of insight Lena realized that Kane also was a profound lover of all that prodigal nature could provide.

'Mostly because of my appreciation of all that's around me,' she agreed. 'Added to this is the peace and comfort of June's home.'

He nodded his head thoughtfully.

'June's done a great deal to improve Mtula Farm. She's a real homemaker.' He was still thoughtful; Lena could not help thinking of Magda, and wondering if Kane were debating on whether or not she would prove to be a homemaker.

Why should she keep thinking of the glamorous Magda? Lena was asking herself when, later, Kane was driving her home, along a lane where water, mingling with the dust that had accumulated in the ruts, splashed up to paint the car with ochre-coloured mud. It seemed that the girl's constantly intruding image would always be present whenever Lena and Kane were together.

'This rain will do an enormous amount of damage,' Kane was remarking, going on to say that torrential rain of the kind they had just had invariably washed away valuable top-soil from the farmlands.

'Yes, Gerald was explaining that to me.' The storm that had raged for over an hour—rather longer than Kane had expected—had ceased almost as suddenly as it had begun, leaving a clear sky from which the stars twinkled, bright as pure white diamonds.

'We're rather lucky in this region of the Transvaal, though,' said Kane conversationally, 'because we often have quite friendly showers—as we tend to call the gentler form of precipitation.' He went on to add that he supposed she had already learned that there was no real summer or winter here, but only a dry season—the seven or eight months of the year when the weather was colder—and the wet season from November to March when, the sun being at its highest here, in the Tropic of Capricorn, the rain reached torrential proportions.

'The air must be very dry indeed during the dry season you spoke of,' she said, her attention caught suddenly by fireflies glowing in the bushes on the roadside.

'It is indeed, which of course makes it stimulating to a very high degree.' A pause and then, 'Do you think you'll still be here in March, when the seasons change?'

'I'm not sure. As I've said, it depends mainly on my getting some sort of a job—and of course, on whether or not June and Gerald want me to live with them permanently,' she thought to add.

Lena supposed that it was only natural that June should evince a considerable amount of curiosity and interest when she heard that not only had Kane accompanied Lena around his grounds, but had invited her into his home to partake of refreshments.

'I had concluded he was just allowing you to roam around,' she added, her green eyes fixed on Lena's face. 'He does throw open his grounds accommodatingly like that, if anyone expresses their appreciation of them, but never has he been known to take the time and trouble to entertain the sightseer, as he appears to have gone out of his way to entertain you. You're greatly honoured, I assure you!'

Lena, conscious of a strange palpitating sensation, as though her heart had begun to beat rather faster than was normal, lowered her long, silken lashes, in order to conceal her expression from the inquiring and puzzled gaze of her friend.

'Yes, I suppose I am greatly honoured.'

'What did you find to talk about in all that time? Kane's such a taciturn man as a rule.'

'We talked about the various trees and flowers; he told me where they came from originally—those that are not indigenous to Africa, that is—and how they came to be brought here. He's most interesting to be with,' added Lena without thinking.

'I'm sure,' drily and with a note of satire to her voice.

'We also talked of my intention to make your garden gay and attractive,' Lena informed her. 'Kane's going to let me have some plants and cuttings.'

'He is?' June, who was sitting by the window, stitching rings on to some new curtains she had made, pursed her lips and said strangely, 'You appear to have made a hit with our austere neighbour. Magda's not going to take kindly to any poaching on her territory——'

'June,' broke in Lena quiveringly, 'what are you talking about!'

'Magda's wildly jealous of any woman who even so much as looks at Kane, let alone who manages to attract his attention . . . as you have undoubtedly done.'

'It's only because of a mutual love of nature—and of beautiful gardens,' protested Lena—but her thoughts had wandered back to the little scene which had taken place when Magda, having admitted to overhearing the conversation between Kane and Lena, had adopted a distinctly hostile attitude towards Lena.

'A mutual love of nature—and all things beautiful, you say?' June's voice held an odd inflection. 'Others have been interested in his gardens, as I've just told you, but never has he struck up a friendship with them because of it.'

'Nor has he struck up a friendship with me.' Lena found she was tensed inside, vitally aware of those stirred emotions she had experienced before. It annoyed her to be forced to admit that she was deeply affected, not only by Kane's actual presence, but even by the mention of his name.

'It looks very much as if it's drifting that way.' June slanted her a look and, with a hint of a frown creasing her forehead, Lena turned away, automatically taking up a needle which June had already threaded.

'I'll help you with these hooks,' she offered, changing the subject. 'How far apart are you putting them?'

Taking the hint, June talked of other things, but after dinner when Lena was strolling in the silent moonlit garden, making plans for its rearrangement, she dwelt on June's words, and wondered at them. Was it possible that a friendship could spring up between herself and the strong, silent man who owned Koranna Lodge? Undoubtedly it was a pleasant thought—but a disturbing one as well. Kane was altogether too attractive, too potently masculine.

No fool, Lena admitted that an analysis of these emotions she was experiencing was best not carried out; the result of this conclusion was an admission that a friendship with Kane could become dangerous...

'But I'm probably being fanciful, anyway,' she whispered to herself as, reaching a low wall, she sat down on it. 'The superior Kane Westbrook would never want to strike up a friendship with anyone so uninteresting as Lena Ridgeway.'

Having set her mind at rest on this point Lena sat for a while enjoying the perfumed tranquillity of an African night, a deep silence prevailing one moment, while the next was filled with a medley of strange yet fascinating sounds of night life in the forest—the fluttering of bats' wings or the cry of night-birds, the scared call of monkeys disturbed in their tree-top slumber, the weird whistles and hisses coming from the throats of animals unnamed and unseen. Fireflies glowed in the straggly acacia hedge; a pair of bright eyes moved in the darkness of the weedy patch of canna flowers, then disappeared again. Away in the distance, to the left of the line of gaunt stony kopjes, the lonely native village could be placed by the twinkling lights coming from the huddle of low thatched huts. The ribbon of the Klein Umgola shone in the moonlight as it meandered past the village, winding through a deep, mimosa-filled channel which Lena had already explored. Glancing upwards, to where a myriad stars shone from the unbelievably clear

African sky, Lena saw, to the south of Orion's belt—and set amid the three stars forming his sword—a cluster of stars resembling a miniature Milky Way. Dreamily she gazed at it, wondering just what it could be. Perhaps, she thought, it was the famous Orion nebula, which could ordinarily be discerned only with the aid of binoculars.

More noises fell upon her receptive ears—whispers from the darkness around her, a strange call from somewhere on the lonely veld, followed by a sound like the ringing of a bicycle-bell which Lena knew belonged to a nocturnal bird, for she heard it several times before. The night-wind in the trees, the distant echo of a drum-beat, melancholy reminder that this was essentially a primitive region of the vast dark continent.

Into the air broke another sound, a sound rising to a shrill crescendo before breaking off abruptly in a gargling cry reminiscent of someone being strangled. A captured creature, gentle and innocent, falling victim to the sharp fangs of the predator? Or was it merely the cry of a tree-hydrax, a creature no larger than a rabbit but who, June had told Lena, made the most bloodcurdling noises at night.

Whichever it was, it caused Lena to shudder, and she rose and made her way back to the lighted stoep on which June and Gerald were sitting, each engrossed in a book.

CHAPTER FIVE

As promised, Kane came over to Mtula Farm to look at Gerald's newly acquired fields and advise him on what to put in in the way of crops which would increase the fertility of the land in this, its first season.

'They've been gone so long that I'm beginning to wonder if there's anything wrong.' June, standing by the window waiting for the men to appear from out of the belt of oak trees that separated the main farmlands from the new fields, spoke without turning her head. 'I hope we haven't bought something that's going to be a white elephant.'

Joining her at the window, Lena was in time to see the men emerge from the trees.

'We'll soon know. I do hope everything's all right.' She also hoped she sounded cool, collected ... she certainly did not feel that way, not with the prospect of meeting Kane again within the next moment or two. His tall impressive figure coming out of the shade cast by the trees into the sunlight, he took on the appearance of some exalted god as he strode with that easy gait towards the homestead. He was talking to Gerald, with now and then a gesture over his shoulder indicating the fact that he was making some suggestions regarding the fields. As the two men drew nearer and their expressions could be seen, both Lena and June uttered little sighs of relief.

'It's obviously all right,' breathed June before Lena could make the same observation. 'Thank heaven for that!'

'What exactly could be wrong?' Lena wanted to know. 'The soil, or something?'

June nodded her head.

'It could be impoverished by all that wild vegetation that's been allowed to grow on it. Also, numerous pests can live in those thorny bushes, pests which can be most difficult to get rid of.'

'But you'd get rid of them eventually, surely?' Lena was thinking of the farmlands around here in general; all had once been nothing but the bushveld, covered by scrub and such things as thorny mimosas and stunted wattles. Many pests must have found homes here then.

'Oh, yes, of course. But we want to crop the land this year, and if we do have pests and impoverished soil then we shan't be able to.'

'I see.' Lena's eyes were still on Kane as he came towards the house; she noted the straight broad shoulders and trim waistline, the firm implacable jaw, the slight pucker between his eyes as if he were frowning slightly, the sun on his brown hair bringing out highlights of colour which Lena had never noticed before. 'You'd have to treat the land first?'

'That's right.' Opening the french window inwards, June greeted the men as they came up the steps on to the stoep. 'I take it everything's okay?'

'The land's not what one would describe as in good heart,' replied Kane, his eyes travelling over June's shoulder to where Lena stood, shafts of sunlight gleaming on her hair, bringing out several shades of russet and bronze and honey-brown which, when her hair was dulled by Lena's being run down as a result of overwork, had not been visible. 'However, we've made a thorough examination of the fields and there seems no reason why Gerald shouldn't crop them this season.'

'Maize?' queried June.

'Gerald wants to try cotton——'

'Oh, but you get all those dreadful pests!'

'I believe Gerald will be able to grow cotton successfully.' Cool the tones now; Lena gained the impression that Kane regarded June's intervention both as interfering and unnecessary. His manner was a plain indication of his contempt for the opinion of a female, decided Lena, her glance straying to June who, although she had coloured a little at the idea that she had been put in her place, was calmly asking Kane what he would like to drink.

The four of them sat on the shady stoep, drinking iced fruit juices, the two men talking about land and crops, labour and prices, while the two girls merely listened, June shrugging now and then, and making a face when she was sure of not being seen. Lena, amused, merely waited for Kane to give her his attention.

This he did, eventually, transferring his gaze to her face and saying, almost abruptly—and certainly with a peremptory inflection to his voice,

'Are you ready, Miss Ridgeway? If so, we'll wander around the garden and see if we can't come up with some suggestions.'

'Fine.' Her heart was fluttering, her fingers faintly unsteady as she placed on the table the empty glass she had been unconsciously holding in her hand, her whole attention being concentrated on Kane.

Refusing to meet June's gaze as she rose from her chair, Lena went lightly down the steps, followed closely by Kane.

'One of the first considerations in this part of the world is shade,' Kane was soon telling her as, standing by a windbreak, he gestured with his hand. 'This should be an excellent place for your rose garden,' he added, saying that the windbreak, being composed of a double row of tall trees, would provide the essential shade needed for the roses she wished to grow. Having told him that she had ordered them from town, Kane had nodded his approval; roses would grow very well in this soil, he had told her. 'Providing you water them regularly,' he went on to add. 'Water and shade are the two chief considerations when making a garden.' He was walking on; Lena beside him. How tall he was! And how inordinately distinguished-looking! Even as he was, dressed in dark blue denims, with a white shirt whose sleeves were rolled up beyond the elbow, he looked every inch the gentleman, aristocratic and abounding with confidence.

'I thought of having this area as lawn,' she told him as they stopped on a weed-ridden path to survey a large patch of sun-dried grass. 'I think it was once a tennis court.'

'I can't recall a tennis court being here in my time,' he frowned. 'Have you asked about it?'

Lena shook her head.

'No. I keep saying I will, but then I forget.'

'It could be a lawn,' he agreed, scanning the area and assessing its size. 'But why not have a tennis court rather than something purely ornamental? You've already decided on one lawn.'

'A tennis court?' She smiled up at him, a wry expression in her eyes. 'Won't it be rather too hot here for that kind of strenuous exercise?'

'Not at all. Tennis is a summer game in your country anyway. We have tennis courts at the Club; I thought you knew that.'

'But you haven't a tennis court,' she pointed out.

'Not at present. But I intend to have one. My cousin, Jennifer, has been wanting one for some time.'

'Your cousin,' murmured Lena, recalling that it was this cousin's clothes which Kane had given her on the day she had fallen into the river. 'Will she be coming soon?'

'Next week, as a matter of fact. She likes to have all her holidays with me.' They had begun to move on again, and Kane made several suggestions which Lena would never have thought of herself. 'You want bougainvillaeas climbing up those pillars,' he said, pointing to the homestead. 'Purple's a rather lovely colour to have near the house. Over there, you want a windbreak of oleanders. I'd mix the colours if I were you. Use pink, rose and red, leaving out the white on this occasion. A whole hedge of white would form a most attractive background over there for beds of poinsettias. I'll get you some of the double red variety—*plenissima*. They have extra large blooms which last a long time.'

'A white oleander hedge, and a bed of poinsettias...' The whole finished picture rising in her mind, Lena looked up at Kane with glowing eyes. 'It'll be wonderful,' she breathed. 'Thank you very much, Mr Westbrook, for all the suggestions, and the trouble you're taking to help me. And more than anything I want to thank you for the plants you're giving me. How lucky I am!' This last exclamation came out spontaneously; Kane glanced down at her, meeting those beautiful eyes that still glowed with the anticipation of achievement.

'You're a most extraordinary person,' was his quiet pronouncement. 'This enthusiasm for creating a garden for someone else is quite exceptional. I admire you for it,' he added, bringing a most attractive flush to her cheeks. Lowering her head, she dropped her gaze and stared at the ground, fervently praying that Kane would not speak for a moment or two. She required time to regain her composure.

On another occasion, while they were wandering around the garden, he making suggestions and Lena asking questions, Kane bestowed another compliment on her which again threw her into enchanting confusion. She suddenly wished that he would refrain from complimenting her, that he would keep to the impersonal attitude which he almost always adopted towards other people.

'What have I said to make you blush?' The question came unexpectedly, since Lena, having turned from him immediately the compliment was voiced, had sublimely assumed that her heightened colour had escaped his notice.

'I—er—nothing, Mr Westbrook. I don't know what you mean?'

'I've just remarked on certain traits of your character,' he reminded her in his quiet, richly timbred voice. 'I said that I find these traits rather attractive.'

'Y-yes,' she murmured, her eyes on the dusty path they were now traversing, slowly and with care, avoiding the small boulders which having been washed down from the terrace by the torrential rains, had been left lying on the ground.

'I appear to have embarrassed you.' The hint of apology in his voice was rendered ineffective by the more pronounced edge of satire. Aware that he was amused by her reception of his compliment, Lena felt her cheeks become even hotter. How would the sophisticated Magda behave in such circumstances as these? Lena felt convinced that her ready tongue would have produced some swift and fitting rejoinder. All Lena could find to say was, after spreading her hands in a gesture of negation,

'Not at all, Mr Westbrook.'

To her surprise he appeared to accept this. He said, a rather strange inflection to his voice,

'Did you know that character shapes one's destiny, Miss Ridgeway?'

Startled by the question, she made no answer. And

when eventually she did speak it was to ask a question.

'How can this be, Mr Westbrook?'

'It's your character which propels you into action. Had your character not been what it is, you'd never have conceived the idea of creating something really beautiful from this——' Kane stopped and spread a hand, embracing the whole sad scene of years of neglect. 'This wilderness.'

'I agree there, but what has that to do with destiny?'

There was a long moment of silence before Kane spoke again. She had time to glance up into his unsmiling face, being curious to read something from his expression. She failed utterly; his eyes seemed almost vacant, and even his mouth was relaxed.

'People like or dislike you according to your character,' he said at last. And then he abruptly changed the subject, reverting to the projected improvements to the garden, and Lena was left with the vexing question: had Kane been telling her, in his own subtle way, that he liked her?

As if triggered off by a nerve-sent signal set up in her brain, the question was to repeat itself over and over again during the next few days.

When June heard that Jennifer was coming to stay at Koranna Lodge, she immediately decided to give a dinner party as a welcoming gesture for the girl.

'You'll like Jennifer,' she told Lena. 'She's nineteen, auburn-haired and very attractive in a horsey sort of a way—if you know what I mean?'

'June means that Jennifer likes horses,' interjected Gerald teasingly, 'not that she resembles a good-looking horse.'

Lena laughed.

'You're friendly with her, obviously?' she said to June.

'Yes; she's a likeable girl. I think you and she will get along excellently together.'

Jennifer rode over to Mtula Farm a few hours after her arrival at her cousin's house. Lena received her, June and Gerald having gone into Fonteinville to do some shopping. Lena had been invited to accompany them in the station wagon, but, fired as she was with enthusiasm for the garden, she had declined, preferring to be more profitably employed. Helping her with the heavy work was one of the boys whom Gerald had said could spend two or three hours daily in the garden, a circumstance which delighted the boy, whose name was Hendrik, since it seemed to set him a little above the other boys working on the farm. Lena and Hendrik were working away, clearing a piece of land of its covering of weedy *opeslak*, when, glancing up, Lena saw the girl ride into the yard and stop by the back door. Straightening up, Lena walked over, a smile on her lips.

'You're Miss Ridgeway,' said Jennifer before Lena could speak. 'Happy to meet you,' she added, slipping down from the horse. 'I'm Jennifer Westbrook—cousin to the great man along the road, there,' she went on with that particular kind of humour which left Lena in no doubt at all that June was right when she made the prediction that Lena would get along with Kane's cousin.

'I'm sorry, but June and Gerald aren't in.' Lena gestured towards the stoep. 'But come and have a drink; they shouldn't be long. They've gone into town to do some shopping.'

'Thanks. I'd like some coffee, please.' With a wholly free and easy manner Jennifer took the steps two at a time, making herself at home as she took possession of one of the rattan chairs. 'You're here for a long stay, I believe?'

Lena stood for a moment regarding the girl, taking in the pretty features, the clear skin, the ready smile appearing in her widely spaced hazel eyes.

'The length of my stay's indefinite at present,' Lena answered. 'I love it here, but I can't stay on too long.' Excusing herself, she went off to get the coffee. When she returned Jennifer was standing up, staring out to where Hendrik was still at work on the weeds.

'Kane was saying that you're making a garden here?'

'That's right.' So Kane had been talking about her ... 'I'm becoming so enthusiastic about it that I can scarcely think of anything else.'

Jennifer laughed and shook her head.

'That sort of work's not in my line.' Elegantly she leant back in the chair. 'The only reason I come to Kane for my holidays is because here I lead the lady's life—waited on by house girls, and with my appetite catered for by the marvel who turns up the most exquisite meals! Kane has the best cook of anyone around here!'

'So I believe.' Lena sipped her coffee, marvelling that neither she nor Jennifer had felt any awkwardness at being thrown together like this without either a proper introduction, or the presence of a mutual friend or acquaintance.

'I don't know if he'll stay when Magda takes over the housekeeping——' Jennifer stopped for a moment, and then, 'You've met my cousin's young lady?'

'Yes; we met at Kane's barbecue.'

A small pause followed.

'What do you think of her?' Having leant forward to pick up her coffee, Jennifer appeared to be disproportionately interested in the milky contents of the cup.

'I can't pass an opinion, not having had very much to do with her.'

'I wish she'd never come here!'

Lena looked keenly at her, puzzled by the vehemence of the girl's words.

'You don't like Magda?'

'I *dislike* her intensely.'

That makes two of us, said Lena, but silently. Aloud she inquired, rather tentatively, if Jennifer had any particular reason for her dislike of her cousin's girlfriend. Jennifer hesitated over her answer, her regard rather searching as she stared into Lena's frank brown eyes. Presently, as if having decided she could speak openly to Lena, she confessed that she was jealous of Magda.

'Jealous?' Lena stared at her. 'You mean ... that you're ... fond of Kane?'

'Fond?' Jennifer laughed at this. 'If I wasn't I wouldn't be here, would I?'

'Well—no.'

'I'm no longer just fond of him in a cousinly way, Miss——' Jennifer stopped and a rather comical frown touched her high wide forehead. 'I can't call you Miss Ridgeway—even if Kane does. What's your first name?'

'Lena.'

'Mind if I call you Lena?'

'I'd much rather have it than Miss Ridgeway.'

'Good! And now, where was I? Oh, yes, I was about to tell you that I'm rather too fond of my cousin—he's my second cousin, by the way,' she added with a sudden twinkle.

'You're in love with him?'

'I could be.'

'Could be?'

'If it were any use.' Lena said nothing and after a thoughtful moment Jennifer went on, 'Kane would never fall for a scatterbrain like me. He wants someone erudite—like Magda.'

'You don't appear to be breaking your heart over your failure.' Lena spoke with a hint of amusement in her voice.

'What good would it do me? I can't have him, so I might as well resign myself to it. I wish he'd found someone nicer than Magda, though.'

'You believe he'll marry her.' Why was that so difficult to voice? wondered Lena. Even now there was a strange little lump at the back of her throat.

'It's difficult to say. But he's more interested in her than he's ever been in any of the other girls he's had from time to time.'

'He's had several girl-friends?'

'He's had four that I know of.'

Four ... Somehow, Lena had gained the impression that Kane had had rather more than that.

'What makes you think he's more interested in Magda than in any of the others?' she asked, and she could not help wondering what Kane would think were he to know that he was being discussed like this.

'Well, he's bought her some lovely jewellery, for one thing.'

'He has?'

Jennifer nodded her head.

'A gold bracelet and earrings to match. She showed them to me the last time I was here.'

A gold bracelet and matching earrings. Yes, decided Lena, it certainly did seem that Kane was serious with Magda.

'Were they for her birthday, or something?'

'Her birthday, yes.' Jennifer took a drink of her coffee, then put the cup down on the table. 'Tell me, Lena, what is your impression of Kane?'

Guardedly Lena said,

'I haven't known him long enough to form an impression, Jennifer.'

'Nonsense,' retorted Jennifer, speaking to Lena as if she had known her for years instead of about half an hour. 'Every woman who meets my cousin forms an impression!'

'Of his character? That isn't possible.'

'Of his outward appearance, and his reserve and that air of superiority which he has.'

'I see...' Speaking in the same guarded tones, Lena answered quietly, 'I must admit that I noted his good looks, and his unusually splendid physique.'

'You sound quite casual,' commented Jennifer after a small pause.

'I don't think I understand?'

'Unemotional,' returned Jennifer briefly.

'Unemotional... How little the girl knew! However, it was a relief to learn that she was not giving anything away, thought Lena, her eyes suddenly caught by sound and movement in the distance. Gerald's boys were harrowing the mealies and singing as they worked.

'One can scarcely become emotional about a man one hardly knows.'

Jennifer looked at her with the most odd expression in her eyes.

'You're the first woman who hasn't fallen for Kane on sight.'

Lena laughed.

'I don't believe that. Kane has much to attract a woman, but he can't be every woman's ideal.'

'Couldn't you fall in love with him?'

Startled by the unexpectedness of the question, Lena just stared, maintaining a cautious silence while she carefully chose the words with which to answer the girl.

'I'm not anxious to fall in love at the present,' she said at length—but suddenly her pulses were racing, and in her heart something quivered. She was remembering his strength—and his gentleness—when he had carried her to the bathroom, then put her into the bath. She recalled the way her emotions could be stirred by his presence; she remembered the admission that friendship with him could be dangerous. 'I'm too occupied with having a good time, here with my friends, to bother my head about such things as falling in love.' These last words came swiftly, tumbling out as if she just had to convince her listener of their sincerity.

But were they sincere . . .?

Lena was again asking herself this question the following morning when, awakened at five-thirty as usual by the sun streaming on to her bed, she lay for a while staring up at the ceiling. No doubt about it, something was happening to her ... something that had never happened to her before. Deliberately concentrating all her thoughts on the garden, she rose, washed and dressed, then went out into the cool bright world where the boys were already busy in the fields and the dairy. Gerald greeted her with a wave of the hand as he hurried off to give instructions to the boy in charge; June called from her bedroom window, scolding Lena for being up so early.

'You've come for a rest cure, and what do I find you doing? Slogging away in that garden at six o'clock in the morning!'

Lena stopped to reply,

'It's far too marvellous to be in bed. The air's so cool and soft! It's the very best time of the day.'

'I won't argue about that. Come back in half an hour; I'll have some coffee for you.'

With the sustained, applied energy which both Lena and Hendrik put into the work, it was inevitable that the garden should take shape, and that results should begin to show quickly. Kane sent the plants on a truck—a huge load of them, including all the oleanders that were needed for the hedge and the windbreak. He also sent some feathery tamarisks and some scarlet hibiscus—these in addition to all the other plants and bushes he had promised her. The young trees were in pots of the kind which, once in the ground, would begin to rot, leaving the soil intact around the roots. This meant that fairly large bushes and trees could be planted without any danger of their dying. Having caught Lena's enthusiasm, Hendrik worked hard, so hard that Gerald decided to give him extra pay.

'Thanks, baas.' Delighted with his extra money, Hendrik worked even harder for the next few days, planting the trees, digging and rolling the area that was to be laid down to lawn, getting on to his knees to take out the weeds from the paths. And with Lena also putting in everything she had the garden was really taking shape by the time Kane came again, this time to the dinner-party which June was giving for Jennifer.

Lena, lying in the warm, scented bath, could not deny that she was excitedly anxious to see Kane's reaction to all that had been done in so short a time. True, the flower beds were not yet the glory of exotic colour to be found in his gardens, but it would not be long before they were, since things grew quickly here—with the heat, the applied water and the constant hoeing in order to kill the weeds. The oleander hedge looked as if it had been there for years; the 'lawn' was dug and rolled ready for the grass seed, which Gerald had ordered and which would be collected the first time either he or one of the girls went into town. The poinsettias, which were already flowering when they arrived, were more than living up to their name of 'fire-plants' as they bloomed in a riotous profusion beneath the oleander hedge. In other beds were anthuriums and allamandas, dainty cosmos, antirrhinums, brilliant portulacas and many others sent in pots by Kane. All these would be in flower within a few weeks, and if by then the grass was growing in the lawn, the garden would have come a long way towards the ultimate perfection planned by Lena.

Managing to put the garden from her thoughts for a little while, Lena concentrated on her appearance. June having said they would wear long dresses, Lena had decided on an off-white cotton with full skirt, high collar and long, very full sleeves ruched into a tight cuff. Dark brown silk embroidery embellished the material which was of a bordered design so that the embroidery on the bottom of the skirt was much bolder than that on the top, and on the bodice. Narrow velvet ribbon, brown to match the embroidery, decorated the collar and cuffs, and wider ribbon of a matching shade formed a belt with lengths of the velvet ribbon hanging from the bow at the back. Her hair, newly washed, and set by June, who excelled at this as she excelled at most things she attempted, had, to Lena's great delight, gained all of its former springiness and lustre. A little colour on her cheeks and lips dispelled the pallor, a hint of perfume, expensive and seductive, a cameo bracelet, a pretty lace handkerchief, a final glance in the mirror.

Satisfied with what she saw, Lena went from her room and along the corridor to the dining-room where earlier in the day she had filled vases with flowers and in addition had made individual flower arrangements. These stood with the silver and glass, the candlesticks and pretty porcelain on the sturdy oak table. Handmade rugs were scattered about the darkly-polished floor; colourful tapestries adorned the walls. The chairs, made of stinkwood and teak, were rime-seated in brown leather strips, and June had made gaily-coloured cushions for the seats and backs.

'Can I take over now while you go and change?' Having entered the kitchen Lena made her offer. June, looking rather hot, but happy for all that, nodded in agreement, but insisted on first tying an enormous apron around her friend's tiny waist.

'All you need now is a cotton kappje and you'll look the typical Boer hausfrau!' laughed June, standing back to survey Lena in the apron.

'What in heaven's name is a kappje?' Lena wanted to know.

'An old-fashioned bonnet which the older Boer women sometimes wear. It's for the sun, mainly, though,' admitted June, glancing at the clock. 'I must fly. Watch the gravy; I've only just put it on. We're having duck paté as a starter, as you know, so if you'd like to see to the garnishings——'

'I'll do all that,' broke in Lena calmly. 'Off you go, June, and take your time. There's no real hurry; they'll not be here until half-past seven at the earliest.' It would be dark, thought Lena, but as there was a full moon Kane would be able to see the garden—if he wanted to, that was. Perhaps, having fulfilled his promise to give her the plants and cuttings, he would have no further interest in her project. But she need not have worried; the first thing he said after greeting his host and hostess and Lena was,

'How's the garden growing? Come and show me what you've done.'

His dark eyes, suddenly arrested by her appearance, swept over her. The light from the lamps, catching her hair, imparted deep bronze tints to add to its lustre; the light also touched her eyes, enhancing their colour and depth. It accentuated the contours of her face, which were already more rounded than when she had first come to Mtula Farm. Her lips parted in a smile as she looked up at him, standing as he was by the back of the sofa, plainly not intending to sit down until he had been outside and shown what progress had been made.

Lena glanced uncertainly at June; the sauces were still simmering on the stove and Lena felt she ought to be in the kitchen, watching them. But as June's expression indicated that she had everything under control, and as Kane was waiting for her to show him the results of her labours, Lena turned to him with a deepening smile and said she was quite ready to take him outside.

They went through the window on to the stoep, and from there into the moon-flooded garden, where Lena proudly took him from one trim flower bed to another. Then they strolled in silence for a while as they made for the 'showpiece', the large bed of poinsettias with their backcloth of oleanders.

'You've done a marvellous job here.' Kane stared in appreciation, while his words of praise ran like heady wine through Lena's receptive brain. The silence prevailed, simply because Lena herself was unable to comment, owing to the little ache of tenseness that had gripped the back of her throat. She glanced up, seeing his aristocratic profile sharply clear in the moonlight. The sense of unreality which had assailed her before was with her now; the stars and moon, the lights from the kraal, the air pulsating with the night-sounds of the forest and bushveld, the inexhaustible charm of starlight on the mountains, the intoxicating perfume filling the air ... all these compounded to create a mystic land, a realm of unreality where, it seemed, humans should not stray.

'Where am I?' she whispered to herself, again looking towards that firm and noble profile. No man should look as handsome as Kane. He was like a god, she thought ... and this could be heaven ...

At last Kane turned his head, and looked into her upturned face, his own an inscrutable mask. 'Your enthusiasm has certainly produced rapid results. I don't think I've ever known a garden to take shape quite so quickly as this.' He walked on; she did not follow immediately, but stood very still, watching him. How majestic he was, with those broad and noble shoulders and the easy lightness with which he walked. Turning his head, he stopped abruptly, waiting for her to join him. 'Something the matter?' he queried as she came up to him. She looked away, acutely conscious of the wild beating of her heart and the dryness in her throat. She shook her head mechanically.

'No, of course not,' she replied, expecting him to walk on. But he made no immediate move as he asked, a curious intonation to his voice,

'What were you thinking, as you stood there in the moonlight?'

'I was thinking about the garden.' The answer came far too swiftly; she was not really surprised to note the sceptical expression which entered his dark metallic eyes. However, the last thing she expected was that he should say outright that she had told a fib. But he did, actually quirking a smile at her as he spoke. Thrown into confusion by this, Lena could find nothing to say in reply, and after a small silence Kane added, with total disregard for her feelings, 'I've disconcerted you, Miss Ridgeway ... and the result is rather delightful.'

She stared, bereft of speech by this total dropping of all formality. It was true, she reflected, that, almost from the first, he had tended to treat her with rather less reserve and aloofness than he treated others—but this ... Bewilderedly she shook her head.

'I d-don't know what you mean, Mr—Mr Westbrook.'

The smile deepened and she caught her breath. How inordinately attractive the man was! Too attractive by far. Lena knew without the trace of a doubt that, were it possible to run from him without making herself look ridiculous, she would not have hesitated to do so.

'You don't?' His straight brows lifted a fraction. 'Another fib ... but I expect it's understandable,' he added cryptically.

'Shall we continue to walk round the garden?' she suggested. 'I'm thinking of June, and the dinner. It might spoil if we stay out too long.'

'Changing the subject, eh?' A small pause and then, 'Which way now?'

'The lawn ...' The garden no longer seemed to hold her enthusiasm. She was far too affected by Kane's presence, by the almost intimate way he had adopted with her ... and most of all by her own uncontrollable emotions. It were as if she were being plunged into a situation which, in the end, was to cause her some considerable heartache. 'And we—Hendrik and I—have begun to build a rockery. Also, I wanted to ask you if it would be wise to put some blue-gums along the extreme edge——' She pointed. 'Along the eastern border? They grow so quickly that I thought——'

'Blue-gums do grow quickly,' he agreed, but added that they had greedy roots and nothing else would thrive anywhere near them. 'Pepper trees are the same,' he told her. 'However, as these latter are most attractive, with their tiny bee-attracting flowers, and the rose-pink berries that follow, you might like to include a few. Put them in the corners, though, and don't plant anything of importance near them.'

After thanking him for his advice, Lena suggested they return to the house. Kane agreed and together they walked along the newly-cleared path which bordered the area that was to become the tennis court. Hendrik had done all the work on the path and Lena was under the impression that it was finished. It was not until she had actually trodden on a small boulder, twisting her weak ankle, that she knew otherwise.

'Oh, my ankle!' she cried, and would have fallen had not Kane caught her, bringing her so close that for a fleeting moment she could actually feel the beating of his heart through the thin safari jacket he was wearing. She trembled beneath his touch, every nerve in her body affected by his nearness. It was only afterwards that she realized that Kane could have instantly released her—but he did not do so. Instead, he held her close to him, in the sweet mysterious silence of the African night. From the dark vault of the sky the outsized moon shed its argent glory over the garden and the fields and the timeless bushveld beyond. The air came alive with sounds and scents, casting a spell in which Lena was instantly caught. Shyly she looked up; saw a nerve move in his cheek before, with an abrupt movement that completely broke the spell, he released her.

CHAPTER SIX

In order to make the numbers even June had invited Rex to the dinner party, and when Kane and Lena arrived back at the homestead the four were on the stoep, drinking sherry. Rising instantly, Rex greeted Lena like an old friend. Taking both her hands in his, he asked how she was, said it was good to see her again, and finally congratulated her on her appearance. Watching this little scene with a rather bored expression, Kane was actually raising a hand to stifle a yawn when June, noting this, nudged her husband, indicating that he pick up the sherry decanter.

'Kane—Lena, are you having a drink?' he asked, quick to grasp his wife's desire. 'Rex, perhaps you would like to give Lena your chair, and you can have that other one.' He glanced at Kane. 'Is it sherry for you?' he said, and Kane nodded his head.

'Lena's done marvels with that land of yours,' he commented, easing his long body into one of the rattan chairs. 'The transformation's almost unbelievable.'

'She's worked a miracle and no mistake,' agreed June enthusiastically. 'What energy! She's never stopped, except to eat and sleep, of course. I think she's wonderful!'

'And her not being used to our kind of heat,' added Gerald, merely smiling at her.

'And hampered by that ankle,' added Kane, looking at Lena. 'It's still not right yet—not by any means.'

'No?' Gerald spoke anxiously. 'What makes you say that, Kane?'

'It gave way just now.'

'It did?' June looked with some concern at her friend. 'Don't you think you should go to the doctor?'

Lena shook her head.

'It was just that I trod on a stone.' She avoided Kane's gaze, reflecting on that little episode when he had caught her to him. Obviously he himself had been unaffected by *her* nearness, she concluded, chiding herself for her own inability to remain immune to the attractions of the man.

He sat opposite to Lena at the table, with his cousin on his right. Wearing a low-cut evening dress of bright green velvet, with long earrings and a sparkling jewel in her hair, Jennifer looked very different from the 'country girl' whom Lena had first seen in a checked blouse and jodhpurs. Watching her, Lena saw that despite the fact of her having implied that her case was hopeless, she flirted subtly with Kane who, if he did notice—and Lena felt very sure that he did—chose to ignore his young cousin's tactics, merely turning away to speak to one of the others present.

Rex sat next to Lena. He talked much, Kane little. Yet Kane was all attention, and she would surprise a most odd expression on his face whenever Rex passed some compliment, which was often.

'Rex is falling heavily,' smiled June when, after the meal was over, she and Lena were in the kitchen making the coffee. 'Do you like him—in that way, I mean?'

'He's all right,' replied Lena non-committally.

'Enough said,' grimaced June. 'It's no use my trying on any matchmaking tricks, is it?'

'None at all, June. I'm quite happy in my single state.' Mechanically she placed the coffee cups on the tray, the action affording her a reflective interlude. She found herself living again that moment, out there in the celestial splendour of the garden, when fleetingly she had been in Kane's arms. Why must his image intrude? Lena firmly told herself that she must contrive to control such mind-wanderings, since they were both troublesome and unprofitable.

With this resolve fixed determinedly in the forefront of her mind, Lena—after visiting the doctor the following day and being advised to wear a supporting bandage for a few weeks, but at the same time being warned not to 'coddle' the ankle—expended all her mental and physical energies on completing the garden. This completion she achieved, with the continued help of Hendrik who, because Gerald was so impressed with the transformation, was engaged permanently as the gardener. Lena, with time on her hands now, found her life falling into a pleasant routine of work and play, the former comprising some work in the garden and some help in the house, while the latter was merely her leisure, which she spent in visiting, or in going into town in Gerald's station wagon. She had dined at Dakana Farm, where she had met Rex's brother and sister; she had struck up a pleasant acquaintanceship with Doris and Phil, the couple who kept the general store in Fonteinville. On two occasions she had gone with June and Gerald to dinner at the Impala Club, and on another occasion she had been their guest at the Yacht Club dance. Kane was at these functions, and he always had several dances with her, but his time appeared to be taken up with the glamorous Magda—so much so that no one would have been at all surprised to hear of their engagement.

'He'll marry her,' prophesied Jennifer just before she left Koranna Lodge. 'And when he does, that's my visits finished, for I can't stand the woman!'

Lena, remembering her resolve, had made no comment, but had put Kane and his girl-friend out of her mind. However, it was not easy, for as time passed and she became more a part of the social life of Fonteinville and its surroundings, Lena found herself meeting

Kane over and over again. She tried to be cool, but as invariably the conversation turned to the garden, she instantly became enthusiastic, answering his questions spontaneously and inviting him over to see how well everything had become established.

'It looks as if it's been there for years,' she told him happily when, a month before Christmas, she and her friends attended a dance at the Impala Club. As Kane had come to her almost immediately she realized that Magda had not yet arrived; as usual, she meant to make an 'entrance'. 'Everything's in flower—and all the trees and bushes have taken root!'

He seemed inordinately pleased with the keenness she was displaying.

'You've had a great deal of pleasure from the making of that garden,' he commented. 'I expect you're feeling extremely satisfied with yourself?'

She nodded, smiling up at him.

'Rather more than satisfied; I'm thrilled with the entire result. Nothing went wrong—even the weather was kind, bringing gentle showers instead of torrential rain which would have washed away the soil before the plants could take root and bind it.'

'You're learning fast—about our country, and its drawbacks.'

'Its merits far exceed its defects,' she was quick to say, and again she had the impression that her answer had pleased him.

And so, her resolve broken soon after it was made, Lena found herself forming a most happy friendship with Kane. He had invited her to watch the polo, he himself being one of the star players; on another occasion he had taken her along the river in his boat. And, together with her two friends, she had been invited to the party he was giving on Christmas Day.

'Life's so very good!' she was exclaiming to June one

day when, after having applied for the post of assistant at the bookshop in Fonteinville, she had been told by the proprietor that her application would be seriously considered. 'If you'll have me—and providing I can get a job—I think I shall stay in South Africa.'

'Super! Yes, of course we'll have you. We *want* you.'

'You're kind, June, and I'm lucky.'

'Kind? Rubbish. We love having you. Besides, look what you've done for us. Kane told Gerald that you've substantially increased the value of our property, that if we ever sell to get a larger place, we shall get a lot more for this than we would have done if the land surrounding the homestead had been left in that neglected state.'

'If I have done something really worthwhile, then I'm glad. But, June, you all seem to have overlooked the fact that I chose to create a garden for my own pleasure—so I don't want this praise I'm receiving.'

'Oh, we do realize that praise might embarrass you. Nevertheless, praise from a man like Kane is really something, believe me. He's the most critical person I've ever met, and that's because he himself is a perfectionist.'

A perfectionist ... Even yet again Lena's thoughts flew to the lovely girl whom he was interested in at the present time. If Kane should want perfection in a wife then he could never improve on Magda.

Would he eventually marry her? Dismissing this from her mind, Lena asked June if it would be all right if she took the station wagon into town.

'I want to get my hair done—if I can manage it without having made an appointment.'

'Certainly you can take the station wagon.' June glanced at her hair. 'It looks fine to me; however, you know best.' A small pause and then, 'Anything special coming off this evening, or tomorrow?'

'No, I'd have told you if there was.'

June laughed and said teasingly,

'I thought that perhaps our austere neighbour had invited you to dinner or something.'

'That isn't very likely.'

'Why not? He's taken you on his boat.'

'You and Gerald were supposed to come too, remember?'

'Yes, I was disappointed that both Gerald and I felt off colour. I still can't think what we ate that you didn't.' June gave a yawn and looked at the clock. 'I think I'll take a siesta. That camp bed we've put on the back stoep looked exceedingly inviting just now when I came past it.' She grinned as she turned away. 'See you some time, then.'

After taking a bath Lena put on a crisp new blouse she had bought before leaving England; it was in a pretty shade of green, and went perfectly with the emarald jeans she had washed and pressed that very morning. Brown leather sandals and a shoulder-bag completed her outfit, and as she stopped for a moment to survey herself in the mirror, she was rather pleased with what she saw. All signs of strain had gone from her face; her cheeks had filled out and so had her figure.

'I'm no longer the drab, half-starved creature who came out here a couple of months ago,' she told her reflection as she hitched up the bag. 'I'm becoming more like my old self every day.'

She was singing as she drove the 'bone-shaker', as the station wagon was called by June and Gerald, along the track which led to the main road. Once on this newer, smoother road the vehicle was a much more comfortable one in which to ride, and Lena leant back in her seat, prepared to obtain the utmost enjoyment from the journey. She passed a huge flock of merino sheep, grazing on what seemed from this distance to be no more than dead twigs; Lena had from the first marvelled at the way animals in this parched and arid land could find nourishment. Adaptation to environment, as usual, she had concluded. An animal used to the lush green fields of England would soon die of starvation if brought out here and left to its own devices. In the far distance, nestling beneath a cactus-crowned kopje, was a Dutch-gabled farmhouse belonging to the owner of the sheep. White, with its corrugated-iron roof gleaming like silver in the sunshine, it was typical of the farmhouses scattered over the veld in this part of South Africa. The grander, porticoed and balustraded stately homesteads like that belonging to Kane had usually been inherited, having been built by the first settlers. Many of them had stood for a hundred years or more—large, white and Dutch-gabled, with lofty stoeps and enhanced by well-kept mature gardens, with magnificent trees to form an adequate screen around the less attractive buildings necessary for any flourishing farm.

The sun, high in the clear brittle sky, was giving out an intense heat and as she passed more animals grazing in the fields Lena wondered how they could live continually without shade. The heat, shimmering over the veld, seemed to writhe, like oil on the surface of moving water. Under a small clump of pepper-trees by the roadside a couple of piccanins in their birthday suits stopped their rolling in the dust to stand up and wave, their teeth shining like pure white pearls as they flashed their smiles at her. Laughing merrily, Lena waved back; the piccanins danced up and down with delight, their jet black bodies gleaming, their woolly heads moving in rhythm with their feet.

Another farmhouse appeared in the far, heat-hazed distance as Lena topped a rise in the road. A squat, whitewashed building with a flat tin roof, it seemed to cower beneath a cover of half-nude gum-trees and a couple of more healthy-looking peppers.

When at length she arrived in Fonteinville, she parked the car and went straight to the hairdressers'. This establishment was run by a middle-aged woman from Birmingham, in England, who had emigrated after having had enough of the humdrum existence of sunless bus rides at eight o'clock in the morning, followed by four hours in the salon, an hour's lunch break with another five or six hours of working hard for someone else to take the lion's share of the profits, then a wintry ride home to her parents' terraced house in suburbia.

'I'd come to the end of my endurance,' she had told Lena on the first occasion when Lena had gone to have her hair washed and set, 'so I decided something rather drastic must be done. A friend of my sister's had been running this place for over ten years and she wanted to retire. I bought it, and I've never for one single moment regretted it. The people here are marvellous; they welcome you so warmly that after the first day or two you're no longer feeling like a stranger.'

She looked up now, brush in hand, as Lena entered the salon.

'Eunice, can you possibly give me a shampoo and set this afternoon?' asked Lena after the two had greeted one another.

'I can in about an hour. I've two appointments, or I'd do it at once.'

'An hour?' Lena nodded, saying that would be fine. 'I've some shopping to do, and I want to call in at the bookshop.'

'Oh, yes. You've applied for the post of assistant, I hear?'

Lena laughed. She might have known that the news

would travel through the small town in no time at all.

'That's right. I'd like to stay here, but unless I get a job I can't.'

'Good luck, then.'

Leaving the salon, Lena went immediately to the bookshop. The proprietor was not in so, after chatting for a few moments to the woman who was leaving, Lena went off to do her shopping. It didn't take long and as she didn't want to carry the parcels around in the heat she took them back to the station wagon.

'Well, well,' said a voice from behind her as she bent to lock the door after depositing the parcels, 'how's the garden?'

She whipped round, a glowing look in her eyes.

'Kane!'

'Finished your shopping?'

She nodded, her eyes travelling to his gleaming white car parked a few feet away.

'Yes——'

'So have I. We'll go along to the Club and I'll buy you a cool drink.'

'I've to go to the hairdressers ...' She tailed off, wishing she had not made the appointment.

'What time?' Kane glanced at his wrist watch. 'It's twenty minutes past two.'

'My appointment's for three.'

'Then we've time.'

She fell into step beside him, feeling as if she were walking on air.

'This glorious sunshine,' she said a little breathlessly. 'I'll never get used to it!'

'Some people can't stand it. They come, then are away again before they've given themselves the chance to discover whether or not they can become acclimatized to the perpetual sunshine.'

'I love it!'

'Is it true that you've applied for the post that's coming vacant at the bookshop?' Kane was asking when, having found a shady corner on the veranda of the Club, he had given the order to the dusky-faced waitress.

'Everyone appears to know,' she returned wryly. 'Yes, it's quite true that I've applied for it.'

'Have you any idea what your chances are?' he asked, and Lena shook her head.

'No, I haven't.' She glanced up as the waitress appeared with the drinks.

'If you do happen to be fortunate, have you thought how you'll get into town every day?'

'I can ride a bicycle,' she told him. 'The exercise will do me good.'

'What about the ankle?'

'It's not giving me any trouble these days.' She looked at him, as she drank the ice cold lemonade through a straw. He seemed concerned about her, she thought. His next words strengthened this idea.

'Do you really need to go out to work? I mean, you haven't any income at all?'

'I have a house which is rented, but the rates take most of what I receive. I've asked the house agent to bank the rest for repairs, and the repainting which will soon need doing.'

Kane frowned at her.

'You're obviously not charging enough rent,' he told her, and it did seem that a hint of stern censure edged his voice.

'Perhaps you're right,' she returned with a tiny sigh. 'I didn't give much thought to the expenses. I suppose it was with coming away in a hurry.'

He looked questioningly at her; she knew at once that nothing of her earlier situation had been related to him by her friends.

'You came away in a hurry?'

'Yes; as you know, June and Gerald were on a visit to England. Well, June asked me to come back here for a holiday. I made up my mind in a hurry ...' She stopped, slowly, as with a backswitch of memory she recalled that the real truth was that June had made up her mind for her. With the recollection there naturally came a vision of her life—the three wilful children, the work, the almost total break she had made from her friends, the forfeiture of any form of social life. How different it was now!

'What were you thinking to bring that frown to your face?' he wanted to know.

'I'm not frowning,' she protested.

'You were,' briefly and, she realized with a little access of astonishment, with a pronounced edge of command to his tones.

'To tell you the truth, Kane,' she said on a sudden desire to confide in him, 'I wasn't in a very happy position at the time of June's visit.' She paused a moment. 'Did June ever mention that she and I were school-friends?'

Kane nodded, lifting his glass and regarding her steadily from over its rim. He was curious, she realized, and wondered greatly that he should be. This was not the impersonal aloof neighbour whom she had decided she would not like. Smiling to herself, Lena tried to estimate just how soon it was before she was revising her opinion of Kane. She did not think it was when he had rescued her from the river. No, it was after that ... but not long afterwards.

'When June came over to England I was naturally high on her list as regards the people she intended to visit. She—er——' Lena broke off, not quite sure of how to phrase her words. 'She didn't care much for my situation—and, being June, she promptly set about doing something to alleviate it.' Again she stopped, to flash him a glance. 'I don't know if you've ever seen June when she makes up her mind about anything, but——'

'I have,' he broke in grimly. 'And if I were to describe her methods as forceful that would be putting it very mildly indeed!'

Lena had to laugh. She saw the little start he gave before staring into her eyes, eyes that shone with amusement. Was it admiration she perceived? she wondered, lowering her lashes in a little gesture of shyness.

'As you will no doubt be able to imagine, then, she had the situation in hand within an exceedingly short space of time.'

'I can indeed.' Placing his glass on the table, Kane added in a smooth and curious tone of voice, 'And what was this situation of which you speak?'

She glanced swiftly at him, becoming baffled by this interest.

'I was caring for three young boys. They weren't mine, so——'

'I should hope not,' he broke in in some amusement, bringing a flush to her cheeks. But they dimpled too as another laugh fell like music into the warm, sweetly-perfumed air.

'They were my stepmother's,' she informed him.

'Your father remarried?'

'Mother died when I was a baby.' She hesitated. 'About sixteen months ago Father married a woman with three young children.'

Kane frowned heavily.

'That must have greatly disorganized your way of life?'

'It did.' She looked doubtfully at him, anxious that

he should not be bored by anything she was saying. She had no need to worry; the slight inclination of his head invited her to continue. She talked for three or four minutes, conscious of the time and wishing again that she had not made the hair appointment. Being with Kane like this was so pleasant that she could have had it continue for the rest of the afternoon.

'So you were saddled with three young boys who were, in fact, no relation whatsoever to you?'

She nodded her head, going on to say that this was exactly the way June had seen it.

'She persuaded me that they weren't my responsibility.'

'And she was right!' He seemed a trifle angry, she thought ... and wondered why this should afford her the pleasure that she was now experiencing. 'It seems to me that you have a great deal to thank June for.'

'Indeed I have!' was Lena's heartfelt rejoinder. 'I've not been so happy for a long time.'

'Not since your father remarried, I take it?' Kane's dark eyes were on her, surveying her critically. 'You were heading for a breakdown,' he told her decisively. 'Do you realize that you're now looking much more robust than when you first arrived?'

'Robust!' she exclaimed. It was not an attractive description but, she instantly admitted, one that the prosaic Kane would be likely to use.

He laughed.

'You don't care for that description, obviously.' Pausing, he watched her colour fluctuate. 'Pretty, then,' he added with a sort of mocking amusement. Yet she knew for sure that he spoke with sincerity.

Her blush deepened. She thought of that glance in the mirror before she came out today.

'You're very flattering,' she said, but he seemed not to have heard, for he made no comment.

'If you do return to England, what then?' he said after a thoughtful silence. 'You'll not have the children, surely?'

'That's something I can't decide. Their aunt has them at present—she writes to me now and then, and that's how I know. However, she did hint in her last letter that they were too much for her and she wanted to know when I was coming home.'

'You mustn't think of having them,' he told her imperiously. 'This aunt must be the one to sort out the business of their future.'

'I wouldn't like them to go into a home,' she frowned. 'They wouldn't be happy.'

'How do you know that?' he demanded. 'From what you've left out, more than what you've revealed, these children were a handful——' Lena grimaced as he said this; he nodded his head and went on, 'Yes, I knew I was right!'

'I must admit they harassed me at times.'

'I'm of the opinion,' he decided after a long silence, 'that you'd better stay here.'

'I must admit that I want to stay, because I'm so happy and contented here. That's why I've applied for the post.' Putting the straw to one side, Lena picked up her glass and drained it. 'There are others wanting the job,' she told him, 'and they've been here longer than I. I believe one of them is a friend of Mr Cookson, the proprietor of the bookshop.'

Another thoughtful silence ensued before Kane spoke.

'I rather think you stand as good a chance as anyone else,' he said cryptically at length, and Lena's eyes flickered as they sought his. She had a strong suspicion that he meant to speak to Mr Cookson on her behalf. 'I believe it's about time you were making your way to the hairdressers',' he observed, glancing at his watch.

'I'll walk that far with you.'

'You will?' Lena sent him a luminous glance. 'That'll be nice,' she added, suddenly feeling inordinately shy.

Kane paid the bill and they left the Club. The sun was still flaring down, spreading a haze over everything. Yet there was a hint of a breeze to mitigate the heat; it blew down from the distant mountains to stir the avenue of palms along which Kane and Lena were walking. Perfumes from the Club gardens followed them, heady and exotic. Lena walked on air, desiring that Kane should take her arm ... or that she might link hers through his. Magda was forgotten; she did not exist in this magical world in which, on this glorious summer day, Lena found herself.

Where was she going ...? It was not the first time she had asked herself this question. But now, as she trod lightly at the side of Kane's tall impressive figure, she could no longer thrust away the answer, no longer deny the truth.

She had fallen irrevocably in love with Kane Westbrook, the man whom June had so often referred to as the 'patrician'. And what was she? A mere plebeian ... so why should he ever return her feelings?

Arriving at the salon, Kane bade her goodbye and left her. She turned before entering, and the smile that hovered on her lips was wiped away instantly. Magda, swinging along looking cool and beautiful as a dew-bedecked rose, met Kane face to face. Slipping an arm into his, she laughed up into his eyes. As Lena watched they turned, crossing the road and proceeding in the direction of the Impala Club where, in an hour or so's time, dainty afternoon teas would be served in the romantic atmosphere of a vine-shaded garden.

Turning only when the couple were out of sight, Lena entered the shop.

CHAPTER SEVEN

'You know, Lena,' said June with a frown, 'there isn't really any need for you to go out to work. You're doing a fine job here, helping me, and looking after the garden.' She paused, eyeing her friend with a rather pained expression. 'Do you have to go?' she asked.

'I'll feel much better if I'm making a contribution towards the grocery bill, June. I can't go on for ever, sponging on you——'

'Sponging?' cut in Gerald angrily. 'You've never done that, Lena!'

'I've got the job, and I must do it. Apart from anything else, I'd be letting Mr Cookson down if I backed out now. He's chosen me from four applicants, remember.'

'I've become used to having you around,' complained June. And then, with that familiar forcefulness that had been practised with such success before, June added, 'I want you here, Lena. It isn't as if we don't get along together like a house on fire! We do! I was so lonely before you came; it's not quite fair of you to leave me now.'

'I'm not leaving you.' Distressed, Lena looked pleadingly at Gerald. 'I must go out to work,' she quivered. 'Don't you see how I feel, Gerald?'

'Yes, I do,' he said suddenly. 'In any case, it's not for either June or myself to organize your life.'

Lena looked gratefully at him before transferring her gaze to June.

'Gerald's right,' she agreed with a sigh. 'You must please yourself, Lena.'

'When are you starting?' inquired Gerald.

'On Monday.'

'I hadn't expected you'd be starting before Christmas,' June said.

'Miss Lewis is leaving this weekend, and as Mr Cookson expects to be busy for the next two weeks he's naturally anxious for me to start.'

As there were still five days to go before she took up her appointment, Lena decided to make one or two serviceable dresses—something dark, she told June, as the bookshop, like all the shops in dusty Fonteinville, was not the place in which to wear one's good clothes.

After buying the materials Lena got down to cutting them out and sewing them; she was employed on this task one morning when Kane arrived, riding a beautiful Palomino gelding, strawberry with silver mane and tail, white blaze and socks. Glancing through the window as Kane stopped below the stoep, Lena gave a little gasp of admiration. Man and horse just oozed nobility and power. Her heart caught as she stared, and as her eyes returned to her sewing she began to wonder if she would not have made a more judicious decision by resolving to return to England. For how could she stay here once Kane was married to Magda?

'Lena, Kane wants you,' sang June from the yard, and this time Lena's heart actually lurched. She made no move, but sat very still, her hands clasped and clammy, waiting for her heart and nerves to settle. 'Lena,' called June again, 'did you hear me?'

'Yes.' Lena swallowed hard, stood up and glanced in the mirror. 'I'm coming!'

'Hello there.' Having tethered the horse, Kane stood and surveyed her for a silent moment. 'You're sewing, by the look of things,' he observed, his eyes on a piece of cotton clinging to her skirt.

'I'm making a couple of dresses for the shop.'

'Most commendable,' he said, but frowningly as he glanced at the cotton again, noting its colour.

'Did you know that I'd got the job?' she inquired, looking intently at him.

'I had heard,' he replied in an expressionless tone. 'Congratulations.' He turned his head as June spoke, asking to be excused, as she had some cakes in the oven.

'Can I see to them?' offered Lena quickly, desiring an excuse to get away. Both Kane and June glanced at her in some surprise.

'Kane wants to talk to you about something,' June told her. 'I'll bring out some coffee in a few minutes.'

'Not for me, June,' said Kane. 'I'm not staying.'

'Sure?'

'Absolutely, thanks all the same.'

'Okay,' she said, and went into the house.

'Is it anything important?' Lena wanted to know, her fingers playing nervously with a button on the front of her blouse.

'What's the matter with you, Lena?' he inquired abruptly.

'The matter?—er—nothing.'

Kane shrugged his shoulders.

'I wanted to see you about some flowering shrubs I'm thinking of taking out of my border. One of my gardeners put them in and the colours are not what I want. As they were put in only last winter they should move without any danger of dying. If you've anywhere to put them you're very welcome to have them.'

She looked up with a smile.

'That's good of you, Kane. Yes, of course I have somewhere to put them.'

'I rather thought so. The land which you thought of having as a shrubbery—that hasn't been prepared, you were saying the last time I saw you?'

'I'd almost changed my mind, deciding to grow vegetables on that particular plot.'

'Don't you think Gerald grows sufficient?'

'Yes, I suppose so. In any case, I'd much rather have shrubs.'

'That's settled, then, I'll send them along just as soon as you've had the ground prepared. Hendrik will do the heavy work?'

'Yes, he always does now.'

Satisfied, Kane looked down at her.

'Am I mistaken,' he said, 'or is this garment you're making a rather dull shade of blue?' Stooping, he picked the thread of cotton from her skirt and held it aloft.

'It's a very dark shade of blue, yes. I suppose you'd describe it as navy blue.'

'It won't suit you,' he told her abruptly. 'What colour's the other one?'

'Dark brown.'

'Brown?' His eyes opened wide. 'Whatever possessed you to choose colours like those?'

Lena stared uncomprehendingly at him.

'Does it really matter?' she inquired, aware of a vibration within her. Was it pleasure that he should be displaying interest in what she wore?

'Of course it matters. Neither brown nor navy blue is your colour. You'd better get something else.' The tones were so peremptory that Lena was rendered speechless for a while.

'I can't just waste the materials,' she protested, asking herself why she wasn't adopting an attitude of indignation at what could only be termed as interference.

'Better to waste them than to look——' He stopped, frowning heavily. Lena knew that he was going to say 'a dowd'.

'I'll think about it,' she promised.

Kane hesitated, as if considering whether or not to comment on that. His mouth was set, severe and grim. His eyes were thoughtful, and a frown had settled between them. He seemed to give a small sigh, and Lena had the strange conviction that he was fighting something within him. He seemed tensed; Lena felt she could very easily have caught his mood.

'I'll be off,' he said, taking the reins from the branch on which he had placed them.

'Your horse is beautiful.' Lena patted his flank. 'What's he called?'

'Chieftain.'

'An apt name for an African horse.'

'He's not an African horse.'

'You know what I mean.'

He laughed then, and the tenseness that threatened to increase between them was gone.

'Yes, Lena, I do know what you mean.' His voice had softened and so had his eyes. 'Shall I see you at the Club dance on Saturday?'

'Yes, of course.' If only her heart would not behave so abnormally! Yet how could it be otherwise, when she loved him, and knew that he would dance with her?

'Do you ride?' he asked unexpectedly.

'I did when I was small, but I haven't ridden for years.'

'Supposing I lend you a pony?'

'You would?' She stared disbelievingly. 'Really, Kane?'

'Really,' he answered in some amusement.

'Oh ... I'd love that.'

'I've a quiet bay mare who'll be just the thing for you. She's a rather charming animal with no vices at all.'

Rather charming ... It was a description she would never have expected to come from Kane's lips.

'I'm sure I shall like her.'

'Come over tomorrow morning and you can try her out.'

'Thank you very much.' She watched him swing on to Chieftain's back and ride away. She was still standing there when, on reaching the end of the path, he turned. She lifted her hand in response to his wave, then she went back to her sewing.

'I've no heart in this,' she was telling June a short while later.

'You haven't? But you were quite enthusiastic at first, saying you were making such a good job of it.' She paused, expecting Lena to say something. 'What's made you change your mind?' she queried at length.

'Kane says that these are not my colours.'

June's green eyes opened very wide indeed.

'He did? And why should he be so interested in what you wear?'

The implication was plain. Lena, vexed with herself for the outspokenness in letting her friend know of Kane's disapproval of the colours she had chosen, endeavoured to pass the whole thing off lightly by saying,

'It was just in the course of casual conversation. He asked what colours I had chosen for my dresses. When I told him he said that neither brown nor dark blue would suit me.'

June's gaze was both odd and disconcerting. Lena found herself colouring.

'Is he going to see you in those dresses?' Automatically June lifted the front panel of a skirt. 'It seems to me,' she continued before Lena had the chance to speak, 'that our austere neighbour is becoming mightily interested in you.' She wagged a finger warningly. 'Watch out for Magda's wrath, my pet. There's a rumour floating around that she means to have him. If she suspects you of competing with her there's no knowing what mischief she might do to you.' Although there was a note of banter in June's voice, and a twinkle in her eyes, Lena guessed that she was quite serious in what she was saying about the glamorous Magda.

'She has nothing to fear from me,' protested Lena, using accents which she hoped would sound carelessly indifferent. June must never know that she had been stupid enough to fall in love with Kane. Life here would become unbearable if she did. 'Kane wouldn't even look at a girl like me.'

'You won a beauty competition once,' June reminded her.

'That was when I was young.'

'Of course it was—grandma!'

Lena laughed, then frowned immediately afterwards as her eyes fell on the skirt panel which June was still holding.

'These materials were quite expensive,' she remarked with a sigh. 'I don't like the idea of wasting them.'

'Bought for service rather than enhancement. I'd carry on if I were you ... unless, of course, you're keenly desirous of pleasing Kane,' June added slowly, her gaze fixed examiningly on Lena's softly flushed countenance.

Lena's frown deepened.

'I'm not in the least desirous of pleasing Kane,' she returned shortly. 'There's not the slightest reason why I should be.'

But, as soon as June had left the room, she began folding up the materials and, putting them into a brown paper bag, she went to her room and tossed the bag on to the topmost shelf of her wardrobe.

The pony, called Something Special, was a dream. Lena, clad in a polo-necked cotton sweater and light green denims, stood waiting excitedly as one of Kane's boys, having already saddled the horse, brought it from the paddock and handed it over to Kane.

'Just imagine her being called "Something Special".' Lena turned spontaneously to Kane. 'Who bestowed on her a name like that?' she wanted to know.

Kane gave a rather deprecating shrug of his shoulders.

'I'm afraid I did,' he admitted.

'For some good reason, obviously.' The pony was standing between her and Kane; she patted its neck and it at once nuzzled against her shoulder.

'Of course. When you've ridden her you'll understand that she really is something special. I'm glad you're having her,' he went on, 'because she's never had a permanent rider since I bought her. Jennifer rides her now and then, but she prefers Phantom; she gets a more gay and lively ride from him.' Kane was preparing to help Lena up; she was hesitant, profoundly conscious of not having ridden for so long a time. However, once in the saddle she felt quite comfortable, and safe.

Accompanied by Kane, she rode carefully but confidently, and long before they returned to Koranna Lodge Kane was congratulating her on her handling of the mount.

They rode out from the vicinity of the paddock, past a trellis of shady vines, to where Kane's boys were busy in the fields. their shirts and hats strikingly bizarre against the green lushness of the lucerne.

'It's wonderful!' Lena exclaimed as she cantered easily on the pony's back. 'This time yesterday I never imagined I'd be riding like this twenty-four hours later!'

'I'm glad you're enjoying it,' briefly as Kane, narrowing his eyes against the sun, scanned the flourishing farmlands through which they were riding, keeping to a path that was in far better condition than the public road running between Koranna Lodge and Mtula Farm. 'We'll go this way,' he said, breaking the long silence that had fallen between them. 'But let me know when you begin to feel tired. I don't want to take you too far on your first day.'

First day ... This suggested an intention on his part of accompanying her again. What would Magda think of this? Lena was asking herself when presently they were out on the veld itself, entering the loneliness and timeless intimacy of a terrain dotted, as far as the azure horizon, by millions of stunted thorn bushes. The ground beneath them was brown and parched; this, and the breeze-spurred movement of the bushes, gave the impression of the veld floating away into the distant haze, through which could just be discerned the purple-shadowed line of kopjes.

'The breeze is nice.' She spoke to break the silence. 'I feel so—exhilarated!' She could have raced across the veld, her hair flying in a shower of russet glory behind her, but she had the strong conviction that so venturesome a move on her part would instantly bring from Kane the stern injunction that she take her riding slowly at first.

'I should have lent you the pony sooner,' he said.

'It's most kind of you to have offered, Kane.' Turning her head, she gave him a lovely smile. 'Thank you very much.'

'It's a pleasure, Lena,' was his quiet rejoinder.

The silence fell between them again, but now, with her mind involved with the scene around her, Lena had no desire to speak. The silence between Kane and herself was a companionable one; she was profoundly aware of this, and she felt sure that Kane was also affected by it.

The sun rose higher; the veld seemed to rise and become suspended in mid-air as it touched the quivering sides of mirage hills.

'Unreal...' She murmured the word aloud, but softly, so that Kane would not hear. Why was time spent with him so often shrouded in unreality?

'We'll return along the river,' decided Kane. 'I don't suppose you've been as far upstream as this?'

Lena shook her head, loath to return, yet aware that to suggest they carry on would not meet with Kane's approval.

'I've been meaning to travel upstream, but as yet I haven't had the time.'

'You're in for a pleasant surprise; there's a most enchanting spot up here.'

The place mentioned lay among an extensive clump of trees which formed an outlier to his forest. It was a pretty cut-off lake—a one-time meander in the river which, before being separated from the main stream, had cut back into the rocky hill behind it, exposing a natural spring that now fell from a bare rock cliff, in a quivering cascade of clear crystal water, into the rock basin beneath.

'It's ... fantastic,' breathed Lena as, having dismounted, she stood against her pony, staring in almost ecstatic wonderment at the breathtaking spectacle formed by the rainbow of colours of the waterfall and the quiet sunlit pool overhung with exotic drooping foliage enlaced by a tangle of creepers and pendulous plants which took on the aspect of wires and pipes and twisted hawsers. Yet from this sub-tropical smother there emerged victorious an army of exotic flowers of every conceivable hue—delicate pinks and creamy-whites; crimsons and blues and sun-polished gold. A butterfly hovered, its blue-green wings iridescent, caught as they were by sunbeams filtering through the foliage of the trees, sunbeams that, on touching the stream, broke into a thousand reflections and transformed the pebbles on the river-bed into multi-coloured, semi-precious stones.

'I thought you'd like it?'

Kane looked at her with a strange expression, his dark metallic eyes roving her figure before returning to her face.

'I find something quite magnetic about this particular spot. I come to it often.' Looping the reins over the bare dead branches of a tree, he walked to the edge of the pool, bending his tall body in an endeavour to avoid having his hair caught in the creepers which ran from tree to tree. After a moment of indecision Lena followed. She wanted to ask about this magical place ... wanted to know if he had ever brought Magda here. Joining him at the water's edge, she sought for words, eventually saying, in her soft attractive voice,

'Do many people know of this place?' A bird called from somewhere above, before swooping down, almost in front of Kane's head. Lena noticed the blood-red colour on the underside of its wings, the long tail and slightly curved beak; the plumage on its breast shimmered in the sunlight.

'You're the first person I've brought here,' he answered, and for a long moment the only sound was that of the waterfall's tender music as it cascaded down the rocks.

'I ... I feel greatly honoured, Kane,' she murmured, a catch of emotion in her voice.

Again the silence fell between them, and a tenseness which even the faraway scream of a monkey could not dispel. Kane turned at last, from his deep contemplation of the pool's clear depths. Lena saw that his expression was veiled.

'It's the sort of place one doesn't have any desire to show off,' he said.

'That's rather strange, because it's so beautiful—and—sort of—sacred.'

His head came round; he glanced oddly at her.

'Is that how you see it, Lena?'

She nodded. There was no mistaking the emphasis on the 'you', but she suspected he had not meant her to hear it. It told her without any doubt that he too saw this place as something sacred ... but she knew instinctively that he would not admit it—at least, not to her. She experienced again the sensation that Kane was fighting something within himself; he seemed remote, as if determined to keep some measure of distance between himself and Lena. It was the most odd impression, and an incomprehensible one as well.

'Yes, that's how I see it,' she replied, her eyes following three small, dark-blue butterflies as they hovered above the rim of the pool.

What she expected in response to her answer she did not know, but she was totally unprepared for the abrupt way he turned, unlooped the reins, and said brusquely that it was time they were getting back.

On their arrival at Mtula Farm he merely stayed long enough to say good morning to June and Gerald, to remark casually to Lena that he would see her at the Club dance, and then he was gone.

'Have a nice ride?' asked June, falling into step beside Lena as she walked towards the enclosure prepared by Gerald the previous day, after Lena had informed him about Kane's lending her the pony.

'Yes, lovely, thanks.' Flushed and windswept from her ride, Lena smiled at her friend, feeling it was useless to attempt to hide her pleasure from June. 'Kane said the pony was something special, and she is. She has a delightful temperament; I'm sure a young child could handle her.' Patting the horse as she said this, Lena could not help wishing that it were hers, for the wrench would be far from pleasant when the time came for her to part with it.

'Added to this temperament she has the looks and movement of a show pony,' observed June, who had once done show jumping.

'Kane did say that she jumps remarkably well—quite fearlessly and with a most superior style.'

June nodded; she was looking at Lena now, not the pony.

'I can't get over Kane—taking this interest in you,' she said bluntly. 'I can't find the reason, no matter how I try.'

Piqued, which was not unnatural, Lena could not resist saying,

'You're not very complimentary, June!'

'You've said yourself that he'd never look at you in *that* light.'

'That's true.' Suddenly Lena felt a sharp catch of dejection; it seemed to block her throat, making speech impossible. She turned away from June, leading the pony rather quickly towards the temporary paddock in which it would be kept until proper accommodation could be made for it. Hendrik, who had been watching Lena from the cover of some bushes from under which he was pulling out the weeds that had sprung up after the previous night's thunderstorm, approached her and offered to unharness the pony.

'Thanks, Hendrik,' she smiled.

'I like horses. I would like to care for this one.'

'Then you shall—providing you don't neglect the garden in order to do it.'

'No, I shall find time to do both jobs,' he promised,

and went off, beaming all over his face, to attend to the pony's requirements.

The dance at the Impala Club was rather different from usual; of the people present two were celebrating birthdays, and a couple were celebrating their fifth wedding anniversary. And so the air of gaiety was increased, and there was an atmosphere of frivolous abandon in a setting of music and lights, good wines and delicious food. Magda, more glamorous than ever in a low-cut evening gown of gold lurex, arrived late as usual, and all eyes turned when as she entered the ballroom Kane went straight to her and, taking her arm, led her to the table which he was sharing with Mr and Mrs Burnett.

Lena, sitting with Rex at a table by the high wide doorway—from where she had caught the whiff of exotic perfume as Magda entered—kept her face averted when her companion remarked,

'There's certainly something happening there. It's already rumoured that the announcement of their engagement's imminent.' No comment from Lena, and after a moment during which his eyes followed the arresting couple on to the floor as the music struck up, Rex continued by remarking on Magda's jewellery—the earrings and matching bracelet. 'My sister was saying that Kane had bought them for Magda, and that they cost the earth. He brought them back from Johannesburg the last time he was there.'

A sudden constriction in her throat caused Lena to swallow several times before she could manage to articulate words.

'How does your sister know they were so expensive?' she asked, simply because she could find nothing else to say. She too was watching Kane and Magda, dancing very close together, Kane so tall and straight,

Magda, also tall, reaching past his shoulder, looking the acme of feminine perfection. As Lena continued to watch her, Magda laughed up into her companion's face. The laugh being louder than was necessary Lena sensed that it was all done for effect. Kane, on the other hand, was totally oblivious of any attention he was receiving from the people around him. But Lena suspected that Magda was intensely conscious, both of the sensation her entrance had caused, and of the interest which was now being displayed in the eyes of the other diners and dancers.

'Rumour,' admitted Rex in answer to Lena's question regarding the value of the jewellery.

'Everything around here seems to hinge on rumour.'

'True,' he admitted, but went on to add that there was no smoke without fire. 'I myself believe that Kane is at least making up his mind to settle down.'

'He's had his fling, you mean—and now he's ready to get married?' The constriction returned to her throat; she tried to remove it by swallowing, but it remained.

'Yes, I mean just that. Kane's the owner of one of the most valuable farms around here; his home is beautiful. It needs a mistress, and who better than the girl he's dancing with now?' Rex rambled on, little knowing that every word he spoke was like a sword point in his companion's heart.

Finally diverted from his interest in the couple who were now moving back to their table, where the waiter was already hovering, waiting to take their order, Rex reminded Lena that she was not eating.

She made an effort, but the food seemed to choke her. For the very first time since coming to Africa she was not enjoying her evening out. She was relieved when June and Gerald, who had been dancing, returned to the table, since their presence seemed to take away some of Lena's dejection.

Ten minutes later Kane was approaching her table, and after having a few words with her companions he took Lena's hand, asking, 'Shall we dance?' even as he brought her to her feet.

'Yes...' Catching her friend's eye, Lena saw the lid come down slowly.

After they had been dancing for a short while Kane said, in a faintly mocking tone she had never heard him use before,

'Rex appears to be giving you his undivided attention tonight.'

Lena shot him a glance of inquiry.

'Does he?' she said. 'Is it so noticeable?'

'In a place like this everything is noticeable.'

'And rumour rife,' she returned before she had time to stop herself.

Kane glanced down, his eyebrows contracting.

'What am I to infer from that remark?' he queried smoothly.

'It was merely a casual complement to what you yourself had said.'

'I don't think I understand you, Lena?'

She coloured, little knowing how charming she appeared to him, with that soft rose tinting her cheeks, her brown eyes so wide and serious, her full lips, slightly parted, so inordinately tempting.

'I suppose I shouldn't have said a thing like that. Please don't bother about it, Kane.' And without affording him even one second in which to speak she went on to talk about the pony.

'June says that Something Special has the makings of a show pony. She says she has the right looks and movement.'

'Oh? And what does June know about it?' he inquired with a sort of cool preciseness.

'She used to do some show jumping. I remember that she won several prizes at our local gymkhanas.'

'I see. And now can we get back to what we were talking about before? What exactly did you mean when you mentioned rumour?'

'It was nothing,' she answered uncomfortably. 'I asked you not to pursue the matter because I spoke out of turn.'

Kane was shaking his head even before she had stopped speaking.

'You'd heard something ... about whom, Lena?' Soft the tone but authoritatively commanding for all that. Lena bit her lip, furious that she should have made the slip. How was she to extricate herself without injuring the relationship existing between Kane and herself? For it was imperative that she should not injure it; it was too precious by far—even though there could never be anything as intimate in it as in the relationship he enjoyed with Magda.

'Please, Kane,' she pleaded. 'I can't talk about it.'

'You haven't denied that you've heard something about me?'

She hesitated, wishing fervently that the music would stop so that she could escape this questioning. But the next moment she was owning that to escape now would not do her much good at all, since, at the first opportunity, Kane would once again corner her and demand an answer to his question. At last, reluctantly, but with resignation, she told him what she had learned from Rex.

'There's a rumour going round that you might—might become engaged to—to Magda ...' How had she managed to get that out? Every word hurt excruciatingly. If it were true that he was going to marry Magda ... if in a few seconds she should hear him admit that the rumour had foundation, then she did not think that she could remain in South Africa any longer.

'Well, well,' he was murmuring, neither his tone nor his expression telling her anything as he looked across the room, presumably searching for Magda, who was dancing with Stephen, Rex's brother. 'What will they find to talk about next?' and Kane stepped out, swinging Lena into a more brisk step, following the music with more care than before. 'Thank you, Lena, for that pleasant interlude,' he said with his customary cool politeness as, escorting her to her table, he pulled out her chair, waited until she was seated, then, with a nod and a smile for her companions, returned to his own table.

Broodingly her eyes followed him, noting his smile as he made some comment to Magda. The girl laughed, and glanced around. Had Kane repeated what Lena had said about the rumour concerning him and Magda? Lena rather thought that this was not so, that he would keep it to himself.

Did the rumour have any foundation? As Rex had said, there was no smoke without fire.

CHAPTER EIGHT

LENA'S work in the shop was not only interesting, but it also took her mind off her own private worries. With the pre-Christmas increase in trade she had no time for brooding on her hopeless situation, or to debate on the question of whether or not she would leave the country when—and if—Kane should marry Magda.

Mr Cookson, having decided quite early that Lena was highly efficient and trustworthy, would go off now and then and leave her in charge—this was usually when he was expecting a lull, such as in the very early morning or the late afternoon. And it was in the late afternoon that Magda came in, just a week before Christmas, her tall slender figure clad in an off-the-shoulder sun-dress of flowered cotton, crisp and cool and enhancing the lovely tan which the girl had acquired on her face and arms and shoulders. Her hair, gleaming like platinum, was coiffured to perfection, being taken back and fastened in a low bun in the nape of her neck. On her left wrist she wore a beautiful gold bracelet; the matching earrings hung low, shining as the sunlight caught them. In all, Magda made a picture of pure elegance ... and Lena felt almost drab by comparison. At least, she mused, she wasn't wearing dark blue or brown, and for this she had Kane to thank.

Having been busy affixing price tickets to some new books that had arrived that day, she looked up with a smile on hearing the light footsteps as Magda entered, and she managed to retain the smile as she inquired what she could do for her.

Magda asked for a book she had ordered, her voice arrogant and patronizing as she stood by the counter, her vivid blue eyes flickering from Lena's face to her waist and then back again in an insolent kind of examination.

'We haven't had that in yet,' Lena told her politely, 'but it's expected early next week.'

'I ordered it over a month ago. Mr Cookson promised it would be in well before Christmas.'

'It'll be in before Christmas, Miss Sanborn. Is it for a present?' she asked innocently, never for one moment expecting the girl to be annoyed by the question.

'That,' snapped Magda raking her narrowly, 'is no concern of yours! You are here to serve me, not to ask impertinent questions!'

Lena's cheeks coloured swiftly.

'I wasn't being curious, Miss Sanborn. The question was merely a natural one, seeing that you're so anxious to have the book before Christmas.'

'Are you quite sure it isn't in?'

'Quite sure.'

'How do you know?' Magda's arrogant eyes flickered around the well filled bookshelves. 'You haven't even looked.'

'I've no need to look,' Lena told her patiently. 'I know it hasn't arrived yet.'

Magda made an exasperated little click of her tongue.

'Are you always as awkward as this with the customers?' she inquired. 'Is it your normal practice to refuse to look for the item which a customer wishes to purchase?'

Lena's temper, which had been rising slowly, threatened to break the rein she was endeavouring to keep upon it.

'What exactly are you trying to do, Miss Sanborn?' she asked, marvelling that she could speak in a voice totally unheated. 'I don't think I understand your attitude?'

'My attitude?' with a raising of those perfectly-curved eyebrows. 'What's wrong with my attitude?'

Lena hesitated, purposely, convinced that if she was not very careful she would play right into the girl's hands. Obviously she was in the mood to pick a quarrel, though why this should be, Lena could not even begin to guess.

'Your attitude is distinctly hostile, Miss Sanborn,' she told her quietly at last.

Magda's colour changed, an angry thread of crimson creeping up under the lovely alabaster of her cheeks. Looking at her now, Lena noted the ugly light in her eyes, the thin compression of her mouth; the transformation from beauty to near ugliness was so dramatic that Lena could scarcely believe her eyes.

'Hostile! How dare you? I shall report this impertinence to Mr Cookson!' and with that threat ringing in her ears Lena watched the girl march to the door and disappear into the street.

The scene naturally troubling her, Lena was not looking at all happy when at half-past six she cycled into the yard at Mtula Farm and greeted June, who was just emerging from the dairy with a large can of milk in her hand.

'Something wrong?' asked June as Lena propped her bicycle against the wall. 'You don't look your happiest self.'

Frowning, Lena related all that had taken place between her and Magda.

'I can't find the least excuse for her attitude,' she added, shaking her head.

'No?' June lifted her eyebrows. 'You seem to forget, my love, that you've been treading on Magda's sacred ground lately. She'll have heard all about the attention you've been getting from Kane. His boat, for instance—he's taken you sailing twice, and someone saw you, because Gerald was asked about it when he was in Fonteinville the other day. Then there's the way Kane always dances with you at the Club——'

'He dances with you as well,' interrupted Lena protestingly. 'In fact, he dances with all the girls he knows; it's only manners that he should.'

'What about the pony?'

'Well, what about it? No one knows he's lent it to me——'

'You *have* been deceiving yourself, haven't you? Servants, Lena,' she added briefly, and Lena looked interrogatingly at her.

'I don't understand? How can our servants carry anything to Magda?'

'All these African boys and women are related, most of them coming from the same village over there; they meet regularly for certain rituals and celebrations and the like. Katje, housekeeper to Magda's uncle, is sister to our Susannah. Kane's been over several times lately to ride with you, and Susannah made several pointed comments when you and he went off together yesterday morning.'

'She did?' Lena's eyes wandered to the vegetable garden where Susannah was bent down, picking peas for the meal that would be served later in the evening. 'So you believe that Magda gets to know everything?'

'Almost everything.' June grinned suddenly and could not help adding, 'I don't suppose she knows about Kane's putting you in the bath. She'll be livid if she ever does hear of it!'

'Forget that,' implored Lena. 'I'm certainly trying to.'

Upstairs in her room, Lena tried to shake off her depression, but it was a vain attempt. She was troubled about Mr Cookson's reaction to the complaint Magda intended to lodge. Yet surely, she was telling herself the next moment, he would know that she would never dream of insulting one of his customers.

Her dejection was still with her when she went in to breakfast the next morning, but if June noticed anything she tactfully refrained from making any remark that could embarrass her friend.

Arriving at the shop, Lena became tensed, waiting for her employer to say something about yesterday's episode. He merely smiled and bade her good morning and she realized that Magda had not yet communicated with him.

All morning she waited, but nothing happened.

However, some time between two and four o'clock—the hours when the shop was closed—someone delivered a letter. Mr Cookson picked it up from the shop floor as he unlocked the door and propped it open.

He stood and read it, and it was not until he glanced in Lena's direction that she guessed it was from Magda.

'Miss Sanborn,' he said with a frown. 'She came in yesterday?'

'Yes.' Lena went slightly pale. 'She came for a book she'd ordered.'

'She's written this letter ... of complaint.' He seemed reluctant to continue and an almost unbearable silence followed in consequence. 'She asserts, quite categorically, that you were rude to her,' he managed at last.

'No such thing, Mr Cookson. I would never be rude to a customer.'

'Insolent is the actual word she uses, Miss Ridgeway.' His rather bulging eyes stared worriedly at her. 'I can't have that, I'm afraid.'

A little more colour left Lena's face. Her hands,

clasped together on the counter, suddenly felt clammy, as did her forehead.

'It isn't true,' she said, distressed. 'Miss Sanborn seemed to be going out of her way to create trouble. I——'

'Miss Ridgeway,' he broke in protestingly, 'no customer would do that.'

Lena swallowed hard.

'She did,' reasserted Lena, but the man was shaking his head. He had known Miss Sanborn since she had come to live with her uncle; she was a most charming person, always so pleasant and tolerant.

'Now if it had been old Miss Stanier I'd never have doubted that she was bent on making trouble, but——' He stopped, tapping the letter and shaking his shiny bald head from side to side. 'Not this charming young lady—no, indeed! Not Miss Sanborn.'

'It seems,' murmured Lena in a flat and hopeless voice, 'that nothing I can say will convince you?'

'Unfortunately—no.'

'Then ... what are you intending to do?' Looking despairingly at him, she steeled herself to hear that her services were no longer required.

'I shall overlook it this time, owing to your inexperience in dealing with the public, Miss Ridgeway. But I must beg you to be more careful in future. Of course, I know better than anyone that people can be trying, but as my livelihood depends on maintaining a pleasant relationship with my customers, then we must adhere to the maxim that the customer is always right.'

Lena looked at him, unhappiness flooding over her.

'I should have thought, Mr Cookson, that already you would have learned enough about me to be sure I would never let you down in the way you're accusing me of doing. It's true what you say about my not having had much experience in dealing with the public, but I do know how to behave—and also how to put my employer's interests before anything else.'

Mr Cookson shifted uncomfortably on his feet.

When Lena arrived home that evening she was again depressed. June naturally wanted to know what was wrong and without hesitation Lena gave her the details. Her green eyes glinting with anger, June said, with a return of that forceful manner which she had not used of late,

'Give the darned job up! You've no need to work for the horrid old man! If he had a brain in that stupid bald head he'd know very well that you wouldn't insult a customer! Give in your notice first thing in the morning!'

Despite the way she felt, Lena could not help being amused by her friend's attitude.

'I can't do that, June. In any case, I don't want to leave. I like the work; it's interesting and congenial.'

'Are you going to put up with that silly old man finding fault all the time?'

'I don't expect he'll be finding fault all the time. He hasn't had a single fault to find with me until today—and you can't put the blame on him for that——'

'Certainly I can put the blame on him! He's dazzled by the girl's beauty! Absurd old fool!' The green eyes took on a thoughtful expression. 'As for Magda—well, I warned you to take care. The girl's seething with jealousy——'

'Nonsense!' broke in Lena, blushing hotly. 'Kane wouldn't look at me in that way.'

'Whether there's a cause for jealousy or not isn't important. The girl is jealous,' emphasized June as Lena opened her mouth to repeat her protest, 'and in consequence she's getting at you—spiteful cat! Kane wants his head seeing to—hanging around a bitch like her. What's wrong with the man? He's managed to keep himself free from entanglement all this time and now he's fallen for a nasty piece of work like Magda Sanborn! Oh, how I wish I had the courage to give him a good talking to!'

'He knows what he's doing, June,' said Lena quietly.

'Rubbish!'

'Rex is of the opinion that they're exceedingly well suited.'

'Then Rex wants his head seeing to as well!'

Lena merely shrugged, dismissing the subject. The idea of Kane's probable marriage to Magda was far too painful a matter to pursue.

It was while they were having dinner that June said,

'Oh, I forgot to mention this yesterday. It's an invitation to a dance and buffet at the Yacht Club. There's a yacht race too, by floodlight.'

Interested, Lena took the invitation card and read it.

'It says a dance,' she observed, glancing questioningly at June. 'It doesn't mention anything about a race.'

'There was a short note in with the card. Mr Burnett wrote it and it's to inform us that the invitation includes our guest. He mentioned the race, and the buffet. Apparently the race was decided on later. He also said that although dress was informal, it would be nice if we added something nautical to it.'

'I reckon it'll be fun,' said Gerald. 'I've a blazer I can wear—and a pair of cricket flannels to go with it.'

'It'll be moth-eaten by now,' his wife warned, then added impishly, 'Why don't you wear a long white beard and carry a trident?'

He scowled at her, but teasingly.

'I'll keep to the flannels and blazer,' he said. 'If, as you say, the moths have been feeding off the flannels, then you can get busy with the darning needle.'

'Some hopes you have! Darning went out of fashion in our grandmother's day!' He said nothing and she added, her brow creased in thought, 'I think I shall wear my navy blue and white trouser suit.' Picking up a dish, she helped herself to more vegetables. 'Yes, that'll do very well, I think.'

'I have a white linen dress,' began Lena doubtfully. 'Will that do?'

'It'll do fine! It has pleats in the skirt, if I remember rightly?'

Lena nodded her head. She would cut out some anchors from that dark blue material she had consigned to the shelf in her wardrobe. Stitched on to the wide collar of the dress, they should provide the 'something nautical' mentioned by the Yacht Club president in his note.

'I'm quite excited about it,' she was saying when, the meal over, the three of them were sitting, as usual, on the cool back stoep, drinking coffee. It was a clear starlit night with the quiver of a breeze coming from the direction of Kane's forestlands. Earlier, while she was washing and putting on a clean blouse and skirt in preparation for dinner, Lena had watched the spectacular sunset of the veld, which held her spellbound, as always. After the splendour had faded in a final blush of pink there came the purple twilight, herald of the night and the long primeval silence that would spread across the bushlands and over the distant mountains.

'Yes,' said June, 'I'm excited too. It'll be something different.'

'The function will be different,' agreed Gerald, 'but the people will be the same.'

'That's the nice part,' declared June. 'We know everybody.' Glancing at Lena, she added, 'And so do you by now.'

'Yes...' Kane and Magda would be there ... The prospect suddenly losing its attraction, Lena had half a mind to make up some excuse and remain at home. She would think about it, she decided, realizing that her excuse would have to be a good one, for otherwise June would not accept it. Lena frowned to herself; living with June and Gerald was fine in almost every way, but always Lena had to keep in mind that she was, after all, their guest. And as such she was ever conscious of the fact that she must conform in almost every way to what June wanted, agreeing to every decision she might make. With a will of her own, Lena naturally found this would sometimes pall, and there had been occasions when the idea would run through her mind that, if she did decide to make her home in South Africa, she must eventually find a place of her own. However, with her feelings for Kane being what they were, and with no possible hope of his returning her love, she rather thought her stay here was not likely to be permanent.

'What I should do,' she told herself severely as she was riding to work in the sunshine the following morning, 'is to be very practical about the whole situation and, knowing that Kane is not for me, put him right out of my mind.'

So easy to say, but so difficult to carry out, especially as she kept on coming into contact with him, not only at the various functions and dances, but in the shop as well. He had been in twice the previous week, once to buy a periodical, the next time to buy some notepaper. He had remarked on the pretty cotton dress she wore, and actually teased her about the way she had decided to please him, by not wearing the dark colours.

'Please?' she had repeated with a little unconscious toss of her head. 'No such thing!'

'Liar,' he had returned, leaving the shop before she had time to think up a further retort to make.

'I almost wish he wouldn't come into the shop,' she was saying to herself one morning as she cycled along, waving now and then to a group of piccanins playing in the fields. Their mothers were working, backs bent, in the mealies and lucerne. They would straighten up as they heard their children shout out, then they too would wave and smile, white teeth flashing. Life could be good here, thought Lena—it had been good before she had discovered that she had given her heart to Kane.

Arriving at the shop twenty minutes before it was due to open, she entered by the side door and, taking up a duster, made herself busy. Eventually Mr Cookson arrived to open the shop door and anxiously she scanned his face. He smiled and greeted her as if nothing had happened. Perhaps he had forgotten; it was generally accepted that the proprietor of the bookshop in Fonteinville was absent-minded.

The day was to prove to be the busiest since Lena had taken up her post with Mr Cookson. She and her employer were serving all the morning and it was a relief when at two o'clock the door was closed. Having the next two hours to herself she went out, into the grounds of the Imapala Club, and strolled about among the flowers. Then she sat down under a tree, relaxed and restful, looking up at a clear blue sky framed between twigs moving in the breeze.

Suddenly into the blissful silence a voice interrupted and, stiffening, Lena turned her head. She was not far from one of the open windows of the dining-room, and the voice she heard belonged to Magda. Lena could not see her, owing to the crimson hibiscus bush growing close by, but the girl's words reached her plainly.

'No, thank you, Kane. I won't have a sweet. Oh, but I was so thrilled when you sent Benjamin round with that note, inviting me to take lunch with you.'

'Coffee, then?'

'Yes, please.'

'I see you're wearing your bracelet and the earrings. They look charming.'

'But of course I'm wearing them, darling. Surely you've noticed before?'

'Have I?' Kane sounded a trifle bored, Lena thought, rising and noiselessly moving away.

'I wear them all the time. It was sweet of you to ...' Lena heard no more. She had no desire to listen to Magda talking about the expensive gift she had received from Kane.

Yet her thoughts remained on the conversation all the way back to the shop. It was very strange that Kane should make that sort of reference to the present he had given to Magda. It seemed so totally out of character.

Lena was still thinking about it when, at half-past four, she glanced up to see Magda entering, looking, as always, perfectly cool and immaculate, with not a sign of perspiration on her high wide forehead, not a hair out of place, not a crease in her dress.

'I've come for my book,' she told Mr Cookson, flashing him a smile. 'Miss Ridgeway said it would be in today.'

Frowning, the old man looked from one girl to the other.

'It won't be in until Monday or Tuesday of next week,' he began. 'I don't know why Miss Ridgeway told you to come today.'

'I didn't tell you to come today,' said Lena, puzzled that the girl should have made a mistake like this. 'I said it would be in early next week, if you remember?'

'No, I certainly do not remember.' Heaving a deep sigh, Magda turned to Mr Cookson. 'I've made another wasted journey,' she complained. 'You know, Mr Cookson, just how far I've come. It really isn't good enough——'

'You've come into town specially to collect your book?' broke in Lena, her eyes fixed intently on Magda's face.

'Of course I have!'

'Why, you——!' Lena pulled herself up just in time. Staggered by the blatant untruth, she had almost called the girl a liar. 'I did say early next week, Miss Sanborn,' she added frigidly. 'I couldn't possibly have promised your book for today, simply because I knew it wasn't expected until next week's delivery. Mr Cookson had already told me this.'

Even as she was speaking Magda was shaking her head.

'No, Miss Ridgeway!'

Lena's eyes kindled with anger.

'I'm quite sure——'

'I'm terribly sorry, Miss Sanborn,' broke in Mr Cookson hastily. 'My assistant hasn't been here long, as you know, so I hope you'll forgive her mistake.'

'I didn't make a mistake,' insisted Lena angrily. 'I——' She stopped, not only because her employer was again about to interrupt her, but also because Kane had suddenly appeared in the doorway. It flashed across Lena's mind that either he had been looking in the window, or that Magda had come on before him because he had met someone to whom he had stopped to speak. He was looking from Lena's flushed face to Magda's cool one, a puzzled expression in his eyes.

'I'm sure the mistake was yours, Miss Ridgeway,' her employer was saying, having glanced up at Kane and then returned his attention to Lena, 'since Miss Sanborn would certainly not have come in today for her book if, as you maintain, you told her it would not be here until next week.'

Fuming inwardly, Lena moved, and began to sort out a pile of books which were lying at the far end of the counter, all of which had labels pushed into them, as they were special orders.

'Is something wrong?' inquired Kane in his quiet, finely-modulated voice.

'No, Kane darling,' silkily from Magda as she flashed him a dazzling smile. 'It's nothing really. Just a mistake on Miss Ridgeway's part. She told me my book would be here today, and it isn't. As a matter of fact, it won't be here until next Monday or Tuesday.'

Kane's eyes flickered strangely.

'I thought I overheard Lena insisting that she hadn't made a mistake?' Sending Lena a questioning glance as he said this, he was obviously expecting her to make some comment. She stubbornly kept quiet, keeping her attention on the books she was sorting out.

'My assistant did deny making the mistake,' put in Mr Cookson, plainly becoming uncomfortable as he glanced towards the door, hoping no one would enter while this little scene was being enacted. 'I suppose it's only natural that she should deny it, but I myself am convinced that she did make the mistake.'

'It doesn't matter,' interposed Magda with another dazzling smile. 'It was not as if Miss Ridgeway did it deliberately, Mr Cookson. Personally, I think you're being somewhat hard on her.'

Lena gasped, while her employer stared at Magda as if unable to believe his ears.

'But you seemed annoyed and angry, just now——'

'Angry?' she echoed. 'Indeed no. I think I was most

understanding about the whole thing.' Magda avoided Lena's wide contemptuous gaze. And well she might, thought Lena, aware of what the detestable girl was about. All this speciousness was for Kane's benefit; she wanted to deceive him into believing that she was acting with the utmost tolerance towards Lena. 'As you yourself said, Miss Ridgeway's not been here long; she's naturally not used to the business, and in these circumstances I'm willing to overlook the mistake—and so should you,' she added almost censoriously.

Kane strolled along to where Lena was standing.

'Do you happen to have a book of mine in that little pile?' His voice was soft, and almost gentle. 'I ordered it about three weeks ago.'

Lena shook her head; she was full up, with tears at the backs of her eyes.

'No,' she said huskily, 'it isn't here.'

'But,' interposed Magda sweetly from where she was standing at the other end of the counter, 'you haven't looked.'

Kane frowned at her but made no comment.

'I've only just been through them,' said Lena, 'to find a book ordered by another customer.' Acutely conscious of her employer's stare, she went through the pile of books again. 'No, Kane, there isn't one here for you.'

'Not to worry, Lena, I'm not waiting for it.'

'I can drop it off at your house when it comes in,' she offered. 'I have to pass the end of your drive on my way home from work.' Her eyes moving to Magda's face, Lena encountered a stare of ill-disguised antagonism, and knew her offer had been the cause of it.

'You'll do that for me.' Kane's regard was kind, understanding. 'Thank you very much, Lena.'

She looked mistily at him.

'It's no trouble.'

He sent her a slow smile, as if to convey sympathy, and also the message that she must not worry too much about what had happened. She wondered if he believed that she really had made a mistake. Not that it mattered, she told herself. Magda meant so much to him that his opinion of her, Lena, was of no importance whatsoever.

'I shall wait for you to deliver it, then.' These added words seemed unnecessary; Lena had the impression that he was still attempting to convey sympathy. This she did not want, emotionally upset as she was both by the displeasure of her employer, and by Magda's spite, which had been the cause of that displeasure. Sympathy from Kane could release the valve that held her tears in check.

Magda and Kane left the shop but stood outside, looking in the window. Mr Cookson went into the back room, leaving Lena standing by the counter, the pile of books still in front of her. The window had a sort of fanlight above it, which was partly open. Lena stiffened as she heard the silky voice of Magda as she said,

'But, Kane, can you trust her to deliver the book for you? She's far from efficient, from what I can see. If I hadn't been meeting you for lunch, I'm afraid I'd have been more than a little annoyed at coming all this way for nothing...'

As Lena heard no more she surmised that the couple had walked on, away from the window. Far from efficient ... Never in her life had Lena been called inefficient. What was the girl trying to do? Lena was asking herself as she rode home that evening.

It never occurred to her that Magda might be intent on bringing about her dismissal.

CHAPTER NINE

'WHAT a blisteringly hot day it's been!' June spoke grimly as she poured out cool drinks for Lena and herself. 'I don't know how you managed to work in that shop. I've been lying down for most of the afternoon.'

'I must admit the heat affected me,' returned Lena, gratefully accepting the glass held out to her by June. 'It wasn't only the heat,' she added, 'but the steaminess of the atmosphere; it was so oppressive.' This was caused, she knew, by the low-lying cover of bulbous clouds which had been hanging about for several days.

'If only those clouds would drop their moisture,' sighed Gerald a few minutes later as he joined the two girls on the stoep. 'We certainly need all the rain that's locked up in that dark sky.' His eyes wandered over the fields of thirsty crops. 'It must come some time, that's one consolation. It can't remain up there for ever.'

Yes, it must come some time, thought Lena as she went off to her room to get ready for the event at the Yacht Club. She wondered if the great deluge would arrive while the race was on, and could imagine everyone losing interest as they ran for cover.

At seven o'clock they were on their way, Gerald driving the station wagon along the road skirting the river. Eventually a glare of light appeared—the glow from the clubhouse.

Finding a place to park the station wagon, Gerald then led the girls through the crowd towards a less congested place on the river terrace, and here they stood, looking down on to the gay scene of graceful yachts and numerous small craft, all with lights glimmering fore and aft. From the clubhouse itself bunting fluttered in the breeze, with small, multi-coloured lights adding a further touch of gaiety.

'Baas—a drink, please?' The waiter held out a tray and the three helped themselves to drinks.

Within minutes they were joined by the Yacht Club president and his wife, and the five of them chatted while watching the activities of the yachtsmen making final preparations for the race.

'I've made arrangements for you all to watch the race from the launch of a friend of mine,' Mr Burnett informed them.

'You have?' June was delighted. 'That'll be fun!'

'When you've finished your drinks I'll have one of the stewards take you across to the jetty.'

As many other people had the same idea of watching the race from boats, there was quite a number of them moored both to the jetty and the bank. Also, there was a concentration of people here, all jostling about, and somehow Lena found herself separated from her friends, and from the steward. Vexed with herself for paying more attention to the nautical activities going on than in keeping close to the steward, she swung round again and again in an endeavour to find her friends.

Time passed; the crowd began to thin. Many launches were moving away, into the darkness of the water, their lights twinkling, laughter and chatter coming from their decks.

'Oh, dear,' she sighed. 'What a flop this is going to be! And it isn't as if I really wanted to come.'

Which of those launches carried June and Gerald? she wondered, in no doubt at all about her friends having boarded the launch on which provision had been made for them. They would take it for granted that the steward would find Lena and accommodate her elsewhere.

With another deep and hopeless sigh Lena was just about to go along to the clubhouse and seek out Mr Burnett, when a voice from behind her said with a touch of relief,

'There you are, Miss Ridgeway! I'm afraid your friends have already sailed off. They didn't want to, but as I promised to find you and see you safely aboard another launch, they agreed to go.'

'I'm so sorry.' Lena looked up in the darkness, trying to read the steward's expression. It was not possible, but she guessed that he was not too happy at the trouble she had caused him.

'If you will come this way, please?'

Feeling extremely foolish, Lena stepped along beside him, wondering whose launch she was to find herself in. Left to herself, she would much rather have written off the idea of watching the race from a launch, and gone along to the balcony of the Club and watched it from there, along with the president and his wife, and perhaps one or two other people she knew. However, she could not put the steward to more trouble; he had obviously asked someone to take her aboard, and therefore she had no alternative than to accept. The steward walked briskly, and in silence. Reaching the jetty again, Lena stared down at the dark outline of a launch.

'This is it.' The steward sounded a trifle impatient, she thought as she meekly came up beside him. '*Wandering Dawn*——'

'*Wandering Dawn!*' she flashed, her heart leaping. This was Kane's boat. 'I can't——'

'Careful how you go.' The quiet yet commanding voice of Kane cut her short. 'Give me your hand.'

'I . . . oh, Kane, I really am sorry . . .' Her voice slackened; the touch of his hands sending exciting tremors through her whole body. 'I don't want to put you to any inconvenience,' she managed at length. He said nothing; his hands still supported her, warm and strong and—she thought in some amazement—just a trifle possessive in the way the fingers moved, as if they had a right to enjoy the feel of her flesh through the thin cotton material of her dress. She tingled under his touch, caught the tantalizing odour of a masculine body lotion, felt his cool clean breath on her cheek ... and then she was beside him on the deck, her heart thudding at the nearness of him. But cruelly into this dream there intruded, as always, the image of Magda. 'I don't want to inconvenience you,' she said again. 'You want to be alone with——' She glanced around. Where was the girl?

'With ... whom?' he prompted coolly.

She blinked in the darkness.

'Isn't Magda here?' she asked in some bewilderment.

'No,' briefly and still in the same cool accents.

'You're expecting her, though,' she said impulsively. 'And I don't want to intrude.'

'If I hadn't wanted you I'd not have agreed to the steward's request that I take you on board,' he told her with a hint of impatience. 'If one can't accommodate one's friends then it's a very poor business indeed.'

'Friends ...' She did not mean to murmur the word aloud, nor did she mean him to see the dreamy expression in her eyes. But at that moment the floodlights flared on, and she found herself caught in the light. Her dress was blowing in the breeze, the hem coming up a little too far for her comfort. Kane laughed as she stooped to catch it before too much of her underwear was revealed. 'I expect you're thinking I should have worn trousers,' she said unsteadily, thinking of June's far more suitable attire.

'On the contrary,' smiled Kane, 'I was thinking how well that dress becomes you.'

Flushing with pleasure, Lena lifted a smiling face to his.

'Thank you for the compliment, Kane. As a matter of fact, I rather felt that it wasn't quite right—as there's a dance afterwards, that is.' The flurry of the breeze having died, she let go of the hem.

'It's very right.' His dark eyes looked it over again, and then his attention was on her face; tense moments passed, with all the activity going on around them unnoticed either by him or her. The launch swayed slightly and his hand reached for hers; he told her in his quiet voice to be careful that she did not fall. 'I don't want to make a habit of rescuing you from the river,' he added in some amusement.

She laughed at this, marvelling at her total lack of embarrassment at the reminder of his activities on that day. Looking back now, his helping her into the bath seemed the most natural thing in the world, simply because it was a necessity at that particular time.

'Is Magda coming?' This just had to be said, but the words came slowly—and painfully. How wonderful it would be, Lena was thinking, if there were only Kane and herself, sailing on these smooth romantic waters.

'She should be along directly.' The tone was confident; Lena's spirits sank right into her feet. 'Sit down,' invited Kane, pulling forward a padded stool. So, even here, Magda was following her normal practice and making a late appearance. So absurd, decided Lena contemptuously. Who would notice her in all the activity and excitement that was going on all around?

'The race will soon start, baas.' One of Kane's boys was at the controls; Lena saw the flash of white teeth as he spoke. He was obviously anxious to cast off. Kane ignored him but took a frowning glance at the luminous dial of his wristwatch. Another five minutes passed; *Wandering Dawn* was now the only launch still moored to the jetty. Two or three minutes went by like an eternity; Lena tensed, praying that Magda would not come, Kane enigmatically silent until at last, his voice sharp and commanding, he told the boy to cast off.

Glancing up into his face, Lena noted the set jaw, the compressed mouth, the cleft between his brows.

Had Magda let him down deliberately? she wondered. She decided this was not the case. Magda had in fact intended to make a late entrance but that, this time, she had left it just a little too late. That the two had planned to be together this evening Lena did not doubt and, had Magda turned up in time, she would have been far from pleased at seeing Lena.

What of Kane? Lena did wish she could read that inscrutable mask that was his face. He was standing up, staring ahead. Suddenly the race was on and the loudspeaker blared out from the bank as the yachts, white sails billowing, moved gracefully across the dark untroubled waters. The moon, low and yellow, became hidden by cloud, and then suddenly the breeze freshened to become a squally wind.

'We're in for some rain,' said Lena in a rather troubled tone.

'Not for a while,' returned Kane knowledgeably. He sat down opposite her, his white jacket standing out against the darkness behind him. 'You're not cold?' He sounded anxious, she thought, as his eyes took in the way the wind was teasing her hair.

She shook her head, marvelling that she could feel so excited, so abounding with pleasure at being alone with him when she knew full well that it would all turn to pain when they returned to the clubhouse, and her place at Kane's side would be taken by Magda.

'No, I'm not in the least cold.'

'Did you ride this morning?' he asked conversationally, and she nodded her head, her eyes lighting up as they looked into his.

'I ride almost every morning.'

'You're an early riser, obviously.'

'Who wouldn't be, here?'

Kane's smile was faint but friendly.

'Apparently you share my view that the early morning is the best time of the day?'

'It's so cool and fresh, with the sun coming up from behind the mountains and filling the sky with colour.'

His eyes flickered with an odd expression.

'What time did you rise at home?' he wanted to know.

'Fairly early, though not as early as I do here.'

'Because of course the sun isn't up.'

'Especially in the winter. It doesn't come light until eight o'clock.' She brushed the hair from her face, grimacing as the wind blew it back instantly. 'Here, one could have a day's work done by that time.'

'Plus an energetic ride on a horse,' he teased.

'That's true. Kane,' she added seriously, holding back her hair as she looked at him, 'I do thank you for all you've done for me. The garden ... well, I'd never have been able to afford all those plants and trees, and I'm sure Gerald wouldn't either. Then the pony. I'm so lucky having her to ride—just as if she were my very own.'

Kane hesitated a moment, then spoke with a certain measure of reserve.

'You'd like to own Something Special?' he queried, his eyes intently fixed on hers.

'Own——!' She looked at him with a startled expression. 'How could that be?' Was he suggesting she buy the pony? she wondered. It would appear so, she concluded and, in consequence, she added impulsively,

'I couldn't afford it, for one thing, and for another I don't know how long I shall be staying here.'

'I wasn't trying to sell you the pony,' he said, his glance half amused, half impatient. Lena said nothing and after a moment he asked, a sudden crease between his brows, 'I understood that you'd decided to settle, having got the job with Mr Cookson?'

She maintained her silence, strange unfathomable prickles running along her spine. For it did seem that in the low intonation of Kane's voice she had detected a degree of anxiety ... as if the last thing he wanted was for her to leave Africa.

But why? She was his friend, that was true, but she was nothing more. He would not really miss her, simply because all meetings between them were casual, totally lacking any small measure of intimacy. The only times they met in response to a definite 'date' was when he came over to ride with her early in the morning. But this was certainly not a regular routine; far from it. Kane would come only on those occasions when, having met her at a dance, perhaps, the idea of riding with her would enter his head and he would say, on bidding her goodnight as she went over to the station wagon with her friends,

'I'll probably be over early tomorrow morning and take a ride with you.'

'Didn't you hear what I just said, Lena?'

She glanced up swiftly as the question broke into her reverie.

'About settling here?'

'That's right.'

She paused a moment, uncertain as to how to phrase her words.

'The post might not be permanent,' she told him at last.

'Not permanent?' Kane looked at her closely for a

second. 'I don't think I understand?'

She swallowed several times, convulsively.

'I have a feeling that I'm not considered wholly suitable by Mr Cookson.'

The grey eyes glinted, but for a long moment he said nothing, compressing his lips as if holding back an angry retort. At length he said,

'What reason have you for that assumption, Lena?'

She shook her head.

'It's too difficult to explain, Kane.' She looked across at him with a worried expression. 'I've been in a bit of trouble lately and it's resulted in my feeling insecure as regards the permanency of the job. After all,' she added swiftly as he opened his mouth to question her again, 'I'm not an experienced shop assistant, so I make mistakes.'

Kane's eyelids flickered sharply.

'Do you make mistakes, Lena ... or are you merely *accused* of making mistakes?'

Another startled glance was shot at him.

'What are you referring to, Kane?'

'When I entered the shop the other day you were denying having made a mistake,' he reminded her smoothly.

She nodded, but went on to say that, as far as Mr Cookson was concerned, she had made the mistake.

'And so the black marks are piling up against me,' she went on.

'The blame on that occasion lay with Magda, I presume.' So cool the words, so totally without emotion. It was difficult to believe that he was speaking about the girl whom—it was rumoured—he was going to marry.

'She really believed I'd told her to come for the book on that particular day.' Lena was most uncomfortable, because for one thing she was telling a deliberate lie, and for another she considered it wholly wrong for Magda to be discussed like this. It astounded her that Kane was not more reserved about the matter.

Kane was about to speak again when the burst of cheering from the crowd on the bank conveyed the news that the race was over. She asked if they were going back to the jetty right away. She had no desire to return to the lights and the crowds; this interlude with Kane, on the river, with the floodlights having been turned off, was far too precious to terminate if there were any possibility at all of prolonging it.

But Kane must be wanting to be with Magda . . .

'Do you want to go back?' He spoke slowly, and after a long moment of hesitation. Lena became strangely tensed, experiencing again the idea that he was battling within himself. If this were the case, then what was the reason? Kane was not the kind of man one would associate with doubt or uncertainty.

'I could stay out here all night,' she answered without thinking. 'It's so restful and—and—away from the world . . .'

'All night?' with an edge of amusement to his voice. 'Now how am I to take that?'

She laughed shakily, aware of the delicate colour rising in her cheeks.

'You know what I mean,' she managed at length. 'It was merely a figure of speech.'

The boy wanted to know what he must do. Kane, after another hesitation, told him to leave the motor switched off.

'Tell me,' he said after the launch had been drifting for a space, 'if this job at the bookshop does happen to fold up what will you do? I mean, you won't return to England at once, I take it?'

'It might be the best thing to do.' A sudden dejection spread over her; it was something quite beyond her control, for she would have done anything to hold on to the happiness she had been experiencing this evening.

'Those children,' he frowned. 'Will you take them again?'

She gave a small sigh, her mind going back to the last letter she had received from the children's aunt. It had arrived only three days ago and it had informed Lena once again that their aunt could not have them indefinitely.

'Well?' demanded Kane abruptly when she did not speak. It was as if he were impatient to know her intentions regarding those children.

'I can't answer you, Kane.' She looked unhappily at him, wondering if he could see her in the darkness. The clouds had totally masked the moon and stars, and the sky was now looking angry and ominous. 'If I don't take them they'll have to go into a home.'

'Their aunt has them at present,' he said, and the implication was apparent.

'Yes, but she's told me she can't have them indefinitely.'

Kane's mouth compressed; she felt that he was exercising strong self-control in checking words that strove for utterance. She continued to look at him; his profile was to her now and even in the dimness its taut outline was visible. He swallowed, and as he did so the lamp from the mast shone on his face and Lena saw a nerve pulsate in the side of his cheek. He turned as if conscious of her stare; the expression in his eyes was strange, but too difficult for her to read. He was definitely fighting a battle within himself. This time Lena was in no doubt at all about it.

'There seems to be only one thing for it,' he said at last, 'and that is that you must remain here.'

He had said this on a previous occasion, she recalled, and its repetition left her in no doubt that he was concerned about her.

'It's very kind of you to bother,' she said with a quivering smile. 'But the decision will have to be mine entirely.'

'There are other jobs to be obtained,' he told her. 'The fact that you might not be quite suitable for Mr Cookson doesn't mean that you have no alternative other than to return to England.' He paused a moment, glancing up at the ominous sky. 'What do June and Gerald have to say about it?'

'They don't want me to leave.'

His eyes flickered.

'Then what's your problem?'

'I can't sponge on them.'

He nodded his head.

'I know just how you feel.'

'The other thing is,' said Lena after some hesitation, 'that even if I did decide to stay here permanently I shouldn't want to live with anyone. I mean, I should want a place of my own.'

'But you're perfectly happy with your friends, surely?'

'Of course. But it's natural that I should want a little home of my own.'

To her surprise a swift frown darkened his brow. But any comment he might have made was cut abruptly by the vivid flash of lightning which illuminated the launch and the water all around it.

'All right,' he said as the boy's head appeared. 'Let's get back to the jetty.'

A quarter of an hour later, with the first raindrops falling on their heads, they were entering the Club.

'There you are!' June came up to them at once. 'How did you come to get yourself separated from us?'

She had not at first noticed that Lena was with Kane, but now she did, and she gave a visible start of surprise. That she was puzzled was obvious by the way her eyes flitted towards the bar—where Magda was standing, surrounded by a group of admirers.

'I wasn't taking sufficient notice of where I was going,' admitted Lena deprecatingly. 'I was just beginning to feel rather lost and dejected when the steward found me again and took me to Kane's launch.'

'How convenient that you hadn't moved off, Kane.' June's tone held an odd inflection.

'Very.' Kane's gaze was directed towards the bar.

'Did you have a bet on the winner?' inquired Gerald, who had just joined them.

'The winner?' Lena looked blankly at him, then transferred her gaze to Kane. His lips were twitching. 'I—we—didn't...' Both she and Kane burst out laughing, while June and Gerald merely stared, waiting for this bout of unexplained mirth to pass off.

'Who won?' queried Kane at last.

'What,' inquired June pointedly, 'were you two doing out there on that launch?'

'Talking,' was Lena's swift reply, and again she saw Kane's lips twitch.

'It must have been a jolly interesting subject,' was June's cool rejoinder.

'I believe it was.' Kane spoke non-committally, lifting a hand to suppress a yawn. He seemed bored all at once and yet, scanning his face, Lena had the gathering suspicion that this boredom was assumed. His glance was lowered, to meet Lena's eyes. The smile she gave him was spontaneous, born of the pleasure he had given her during the past hour and a half. She was not to know it, but it was the most disarming smile, and one which deeply affected its recipient. His glance straying to Magda, an inscrutable expression entered his eyes. 'Please excuse me,' he said with an abruptness that startled all three of his companions. 'I'll see you later.' And with that he strode away towards the bar. Lena's spirits sank right down to the depths, yet she contrived to retain her smile as Rex, coming breezily up to her, asked her to dance.

'What a race!' he was exclaiming the next moment. 'Did you have a flutter?'

'No,' she returned briefly, twisting her head to pick out Kane and his partner, who were just stepping on to the dance floor.

'Good thing the storm kept off. It's certainly sending it down now.'

'It's desperately needed.' Lena's eye caught that of Magda; there was something akin to venom on the girl's beautiful face. Yet a dazzling smile transformed the features as, turning, Magda looked up into her partner's face, and answered something he had said to her.

'Magda watched the race from the veranda,' Rex said, having noticed that Lena was looking at the girl. 'She arrived just too late to catch Kane's launch. I wouldn't have thought he'd go off without her. However, I expect he was teaching her a lesson for always being late.' A pause and then, 'It couldn't have been much fun for him, though, watching the race all by himself.'

Lena said nothing; she was not in the mood for talking anyway. The remainder of the evening could only be an anticlimax and she wondered how she would manage to get through it, caught as she was in this depressing state of bathos.

But, much to her astonishment, Kane was not totally absorbed with the glamorous Magda after all. He approached her as she mingled with those who were standing by the buffet tables, an empty plate in her hand.

'Are you spoilt for choice?' The cool but friendly voice at her elbow brought her round with eager speed, her heart leaping. Colour touched her cheeks, caressingly, and her lovely brown eyes lighted up. All this was spontaneous, out of her control. Kane, so tall and distinguished-looking in his outfit of navy blue and white, stood staring enigmatically into her face, taking in all the unaffected beauty, the smile that began quivering, hesitantly, before it blossomed out to something so attractive that he actually caught his breath.

'I'm not hungry,' she replied, fervently hoping that she was managing to keep hidden the tumult which raged within her.

'Not hungry?' in some considerable surprise. 'You must be, after that sail out there, on the breezy river.'

She wondered what he would say if she told him that he himself was the real cause of her lost appetite. Instead she asked,

'Are you intending to eat, Kane?'

'Of course.'

Her eyes naturally flickered around. Where was Magda?

'You're ... you're eating with ... someone else?' He must know whom she meant, thought Lena, blushing as this struck her.

'I'm eating with you,' was the unexpected reply from Kane. 'That is,' he added with a hint of anxiety that was quite obviously feigned, 'if you'll have me?'

She smiled adorably.

'I'll love having you,' she murmured shyly, and averted her head in order to conceal her expression from those perceptive eyes of his.

'Well said.' He took up a plate. 'What about some of

these savouries?' he suggested, himself forking up a couple of meat pasties and a corn fritter to go with them.

Lena, still undecided, moved along beside him until she came to the sandwiches. She took two, and some garnishings of green salad.

'Is that all?' Kane looked severely at her. 'You can always come again,' he added, turning his head to seek for a table. 'Over here.'

They sat near a window, looking out on to a garden which, despite its floodlighting, looked exceedingly forlorn and miserable. The torrential rain had ceased but the more gentle precipitation continued. Now and then the sky would be lit with the blue-white flash of lightning, and thunder would roll in the distance.

'Are you enjoying yourself?' inquired Kane after a long—and not altogether comfortable—silence had dropped between them.

'Yes, of course.' This was the truth, but had he asked the question ten minutes ago she would have been forced to lie.

'I see your old friend Rex was soon in attendance.'

Involuntarily, Lena shot him a questioning glance. 'He invited me to dance with him, yes.'

'He's the most eligible young man around here.'

'What about you——?' This came out before she could prevent it and, confusion sweeping over her, she averted her head, taking a bite out of one of her sandwiches while nervously toying with a crisp green lettuce leaf.

'Am I eligible?' queried Kane in some amusement.

'I——' She stopped, irresolute, while she attempted to find something to say. She failed to do so and decided that candour was her only course. 'I expect people here regard you as eligible,' she said.

'And I wonder how they regard you?' he returned,

deftly veering the conversation from himself. 'You're a most attractive girl, Lena.'

She coloured adorably.

'Thank you,' she murmured in quiet, demure accents.

'If you were to find yourself a husband,' he said slowly, 'it would solve all your problems.'

Find herself a husband . . . So casually he had uttered those words, and as she repeated them to herself a spasm of pain shot through her whole body. Kane, it appeared, would prefer that she marry, just in order that she could remain here—and continue to be his friend. As to *whom* she married—well, that was a matter of total indifference to him, obviously.

Steadying herself against this indifference, she managed eventually to speak.

'I have no intention of marrying for the sole purpose of solving my immediate problems,' she replied, her tones constrained. 'That would be the height of folly——' She stopped a moment before adding, 'I think you will agree with me about that?'

'I've offended you, haven't I?' he said, bypassing her question.

'It doesn't matter.' Her voice caught and she turned away. How easily this man could affect her mood, bringing her happiness one moment and sheer undiluted misery the next. Of course, he was not to know how painfully his words had wrenched at her heart, much less was he to know that the only man she would be glad to marry was Kane himself.

'If I've offended you it certainly does matter. I'm sorry, Lena.'

She shook her head.

'There isn't anything to apologize for, Kane.'

Gently he took her plate from her.

'It's obvious that you don't want this,' he said, and

placed it on top of his empty one. 'Come on, let's dance!'

This was better, she thought, as she slipped into his arms. The music was a waltz, slow and haunting. Once, she caught the invidious glance of Kane's girl-friend, but somehow it flowed off her without leaving any impression. This moment was far too precious for any intrusion to be allowed to mar it.

'We'll go outside,' said Kane as they reached the open window. 'The smell of the veld after rain is one of those things that I never like to miss.'

'The appreciation of nature again,' she murmured, totally at ease now as she stepped out, first on to the verandah and then down into the garden itself. 'The stars are coming back,' she added, looking up into the velvet sky.

'They were there all the time,' he teased.

'You know what I mean.' She fell into step beside him as he strolled away from the sounds of music coming from the ballroom. 'Oh, but it's beautiful now that the rain's stopped!' She inhaled deeply, taking in a heady draught of pure cool air. 'I shall miss it all if I do decide to go home,' she could not help saying on a little dejected note.

'There's really no need to think of that, Lena.' He spoke softly, and with a sort of grim concern that filled her with a deep yearning for him, for the bliss of his arms about her, the ecstasy that would result from the touch of his lips on hers. How she envied Magda!

'I'll not think of it just now,' she promised immediately. 'The night's far too enjoyable to spoil it by worrying about the future.'

'It's enjoyable for you, too?' Again that soft tone, but there was something else in it which she failed to understand.

'Too?' she repeated, her senses responding to the

implication of this one small word. 'So you are happy, too, it would seem?'

He glanced down into her face and said,

'I'm happy, yes.' He paused a moment, and then, a most curious inflection in his voice, 'Tell me, Lena, were you glad it was my boat you boarded this evening?'

The unexpectedness of the question took her completely by surprise, and she was some seconds in replying.

'Why, yes, of course I was glad, Kane.' He said nothing, appearing to be considering this and after a moment she added, 'I felt—at first, that was—that I might be inconveniencing you.'

'In what way?' he inquired disconcertingly.

'You weren't expecting to have me on board, for one thing.'

'Do you think that made any difference?' He looked down at her and smiled. 'Surely you know I wouldn't mind having you on board?'

She flushed enchantingly and shook her head, convinced that even if Magda had been there with him he would still have welcomed her, Lena, on to his launch.

'Yes, I did know that you wouldn't mind.'

'It was a pleasure, I assure you, my dear.'

My dear ... This was not the first time he had used these two words. They did not mean a thing, yet she derived a certain degree of pleasure from hearing them.

Having reached an avenue of ancient oak trees they stepped into a tunnel of incalculable gloom. Soon all was inky blackness, and instinctively Lena moved close to her companion who, on sudden impulse, took hold of her hand and held it tightly as they walked along in silence.

Lena quivered at his touch, wishing she could curl

her fingers lovingly around his, but instead she was forced to keep a cautious restraint on her emotions, lest she give away her secret. She supposed she could have pulled her hand away, but the temptation to be close to him was far too great.

'What are you thinking about?' Kane's voice, strangely vibrant, and with an inflection that was almost tender, broke rather gently into her musings and she turned her head, lifting it automatically to cast him a sideways glance. In the blackness all she saw was the indeterminate line of his profile.

'It was nothing of importance,' she lied.

'You don't mind being out here with me ... in the dark?'

The question startled her, as several of his questions had startled her of late. He was a most strange man, she concluded, wishing she could understand why, on some occasions, he would be coolly impersonal, on others, warm, as a good friend should be, and on other occasions, almost intimate ... as he was now.

'I—I h-hadn't th-thought much about it,' she replied at length, having been prompted by a repetition of his query.

He laughed softly, and to her amazement she felt his fingers curl round hers. As always, when she was alone with Kane, there intruded the image of Magda. This time it brought with it the inevitable question: why wasn't Kane with the girl? True, at these functions it was usual for everyone to mix, rather than for a couple to keep together in intimate isolation. But that Kane should have brought her out here instead of his girl-friend was a circumstance which Lena quite naturally found most puzzling.

And what of the girl herself? What were her feelings at this time? She had seen Kane and Lena dancing together; her eyes must inevitably have sought for them as the dance progressed. So she would know that both were missing from the ballroom ... and she would quite naturally conclude that they were together.

Kane's fingers still held Lena's even when they emerged from the darkness of the avenue, his hand falling to his side only when, having walked towards the clubhouse, they could be seen by the people within. Reaching the veranda, Kane stopped, and stood for a long moment gazing down at his lovely companion, taking in the teased condition of her hair, the flush of her cheeks, the full, slightly parted lips. Noting the flickering of his eyes, Lena did wonder if he were finding her attractive, and because it was such a pleasant thought, a lovely smile fluttered to her lips. Kane's whole manner seemed to change; it was as if he froze within himself. He turned away, and she knew that this action was deliberate, made because he no longer had any desire to look at her. Why should this be? she asked herself. Suddenly she wanted to question him, to ask what was wrong, but a terrible little lump settled in her throat, obstructing the words she wanted to speak.

'We'd best be going inside.' Kane's cool impersonal voice was like a dagger in her heart. 'We've been out here far too long.'

'Are, there you are!' exclaimed Magda, as Kane and Lena stepped from the veranda into the brilliantly-lighted ballroom. 'The Van de Westhuisens want us to join them at the bar. It's Maria's birthday and they're opening a bottle of champagne.' As she spoke Kane had turned aside, to answer a question being put to him by Mr Burnett. Seizing the opportunity, Magda sent Lena a glance of sheer hatred. 'Keep away from Kane,' she just had time to say before he turned again, the president having moved away. 'So we'd better be going, darling.'

'Of course.' He turned a set unsmiling countenance towards Lena. 'Please excuse me,' he said and, tucking Magda's arm into his, he went with her to the bar.

CHAPTER TEN

WITH less than a week to go before Christmas the shop was more busy than ever, people coming from far and wide to collect books they had previously ordered, or to browse through those which Mr Cookson kept in stock. In addition to books, many other commodities were offered for sale at this time of the year—from small toys and games to decorations for the home and lights for the Christmas tree.

'I can't get used to the fact of high summer being in December,' Lena said ruefully to Mr Cookson when, the temperature that day having reached a hundred in the shade, she was experiencing the utmost difficulty in maintaining a cool appearance as she busied herself with the customers.

'No, it must be very new to you, being used to Christmas coming in midwinter.' Turning away to serve a customer, he left Lena to serve Rex, who had just entered with his sister. Lena chatted with them, as was her normal practice as she served the customers. In addition to buying several books, Rex bought gifts for the tree and a couple of games for the child of a friend of his. As several people were browsing around Lena did not notice Magda until she heard her voice, slightly raised, asking Mr Cookson how much longer she would have to wait.

'Miss Ridgeway appears to be spending the whole of the afternoon on one customer,' she added on a querulous note. 'I hate complaining about anyone, but I do consider I have a complaint on this occasion.'

Lena and Rex exchanged glances.

'What's got into her?' he asked, frowning.

Lena, pale but composed, looked at Magda and said politely,

'Have you come to collect your book?'

'If it's here, yes.'

'It's been here since Tuesday.' She looked at Rex, who, with his sister, was examining a set of coloured lights. 'Do you mind if I serve Miss Sanborn?'

'Serve her by all means,' he recommended, and it was in a voice which the girl could quite easily pick up. 'And let her go,' he added, this time in a whisper. But as she was watching him intently Magda knew that he had said something which he had not intended for her ears. Her mouth set tightly and her eyes, moving from Rex's profile, stared arrogantly into Lena's. Stooping, Lena took the book from under the counter, wrapped it up and, handing it over, waited to take the money.

'It goes on my account,' snapped Magda, looking superciliously at her.

'Very well.' But Lena glanced at Mr Cookson, just to make sure this was correct.

Nodding his head, he opened a drawer, extracted a ledger, and handed it over to her.

'You enter it in there,' he said, returning his attention to his own customer.

'I take it that you've examined the book, just to make sure it's in perfect condition?' Magda's voice had an imperious ring that served to make Lena's hackles rise.

'Certainly I have, Miss Sanborn,' she assured her coldly.

'So long as I have your guarantee, Miss Ridgeway,' she said and, turning, left the shop.

'A nasty piece of work if ever there was one,' declared Rex disgustedly. 'I wonder what made her adopt an attitude like that?' He looked curiously at

Lena. 'It's more than plain that she doesn't like you,' he said.

'She's never liked me.' Automatically Lena produced another box of fairy lights, slightly larger than those at which Rex was looking. 'What about these? They seem to be better value for money to me.' Her words were as automatic as her actions, for she could not get Magda out of her mind. It was obvious that she was insanely jealous of Lena's friendship with Kane—yet she need not have been, thought Lena broodingly. The friendship was purely platonic, and likely to remain that way until the time when Lena decided to leave the country. After that—well, she did not expect there would be much correspondence between Kane and herself. He would be too busy to write, or perhaps he would decide that it was just a waste of time anyway, seeing that Lena would not be visiting South Africa again.

She gave a deep sigh, and for the rest of the day she was unable to shake off her dejection.

'I don't know what's wrong with me,' she was saying as she cycled home in the sunshine. 'I feel that something dreadful is hanging over me.'

She was soon to know, her first customer the following morning being Magda, who was returning the book. Mr Cookson was not yet in the shop, but the girl demanded to see him, her tone so loud and imperative that it was bound to reach him in the room behind the shop where he was having his breakfast.

'What's wrong?' Lena's eyes were on the parcel which Magda had under her arm. 'You say you're not willing to have the book.' She held out her hand, but Magda refused to relinquish the parcel.

'It's in a disgraceful condition!' Magda's glance was haughty and accusing. 'You said it was perfect, that you'd examined it!'

'And so I did examine it.' Lena's nerves were tensed; she had no doubts at all that some damage had been done to the book, which was a most expensive one, and which certainly could not be replaced before Christmas. 'There was nothing at all wrong with it.'

A sneer curved Magda's lips.

'Except what you did—either by accident or design, Miss Ridgeway!'

'You believe that I would damage a book?' Lena shook her head. 'How little you know me, Miss Sanborn. The very fact that someone has gone to all the trouble of writing it, and probably painstakingly going over it again and again—this is more than enough for me to want to treasure a book. I would never deliberately deface one.' She thought of her own modest library; every book was almost as new, even those she had read over and over again.

'Naturally you'll make excuses,' snapped the girl, her arrogant eyes raking Lena contemptuously. 'But you know what you've done—— Ah, Mr Cookson,' she said, turning as he entered the shop. 'Take a look at this book!' She threw it on to the counter in front of him. 'I'm certainly not paying for it! You can order me another—but only if you can get it before Christmas!'

He shook his head, his eyes wandering vaguely from Lena's pale and troubled features to the arrogant face of the girl on the other side of the counter.

'It's too late for that, Miss Sanborn,' he muttered, opening the parcel with slow, cumbersome movements. Both girls watched silently as he took out the book. 'It looks all right to me,' he pronounced, his worried frown disappearing like magic. 'What's the nature of your complaint, Miss Sanborn——?'

'Inside, Mr Cookson,' interrupted Magda rudely, and without affording him the chance to open the book she snatched it from his hands and flipped back the first few pages. 'There!' She pushed the book at him, heard him gasp as he turned to his assistant.

'It's ink, Miss Ridgeway ... from your fountain pen.'

Swallowing convulsively, Lena shook her head.

'I know I use my fountain pen to fill in the labels which I attach to the special orders, Mr Cookson, but I didn't get ink all over the inside of the book like this.'

'Your pen leaked,' broke in Magda. 'That's plain for anyone to see.' Turning to Mr Cookson, she said, 'Perhaps you consider it was natural that she should try to hide what she had done? I personally would have owned up at once, being quite prepared to pay for the book.'

The old man sighed.

'All I can say is that I'm sorry, Miss Sanborn, and that of course I shall not include it on your account——'

'I should hope you wouldn't!'

'As for a replacement...' Again he shook his head. 'That isn't possible until the New Year, as you must understand, Miss Sanborn?'

'All I understand,' she told him icily, 'is that the person for whom I was purchasing that book is not going to get his Christmas present!'

'Yes ... well, for that I am deeply sorry,' repeated Mr Cookson with another despondent sigh.

Lena received her notice with equanimity, since she had half expected it even before this latest piece of malice had brought her even lower in her employer's estimation. The fact that she had to leave was not important in itself, since she had almost become resigned to the idea of returning to England after Christmas. What was important to her was that Magda would be sure to spread it around that she had been dismissed for incompetence—for defacing a book and then selling it—this to avoid having to pay for it.

'If you'd like me to leave at once,' she said to Mr Cookson that evening as she tidied up the shop prior to going home, 'I'll do so.'

'No ... I can't get anyone else in, and I am very busy, as you know.' He looked sadly at her. 'At first, Miss Ridgeway, you were so very efficient and trustworthy that I had no anxiety whatsoever in leaving you in charge. In fact, I thanked Mr Westbrook more than once for persuading me to take you on.'

In the act of putting some heavy volumes away on a shelf, Lena turned, the books in her hands.

'Mr Westbrook recommended me?' She had suspected this, she recalled.

The old man nodded his head.

'Not only recommended, but almost bullied me into taking you on—— Oh, not in any nasty way, you understand? But he stood here in my shop and I soon realized that he wasn't intending to leave until I'd given him my promise that I'd give you a trial. And, as I said just now, you proved to be excellent. I can't think what's happened to change you. It's a pity, and Mr Westbrook's not going to be pleased, but I can't have these complaints keep coming in, can I?'

'They've come from one person only, Mr Cookson.'

'True. But they've been valid complaints.' He looked intently at her. 'I'm wondering if you have a grudge against her, Miss Ridgeway?'

Lena put the books away, then turned again; she was pale and her pulse was speeding. She felt almost sick with dejection, yet she answered him calmly, amazed at the steadiness of her voice,

'No, Mr Cookson, I have no grudge against Miss Sanborn. It's she who has a grudge against me. However, you, as the proprietor of this establishment, have the right to dispense with my services, as you are doing.' She paused a moment. 'Mr Westbrook's book's here. I promised to deliver it?' She stopped and looked at him, a question in her silence. He nodded his head.

'Take it by all means, Miss Ridgeway,' he said.

It was almost dusk when Lena turned her bicycle into the long, tree-shaded drive leading up to Koranna Lodge. She had just been on the point of closing the shop when two people entered and she was kept another half hour while they waded, with dilatory indecision, through a stack of children's books. They left without having made a purchase, leaving Lena to begin tidying up all over again.

That she was looking tired and despondent was only to be expected; that Kane should immediately notice was also to be expected since, right from the first, he had evinced an inexplicable interest in her appearance.

'Something wrong?' he inquired, his keen eyes examining her pale face, the tired lines beneath her eyes and the quivering of her mouth.

She shook her head, loath to speak about his girlfriend. And yet on the other hand she felt she owed it to him to explain, since it had been he who had got the job for her in the first place.

'I—I've got the s-sack——' Without warning the tears came, released by the emotion within her and the concern portrayed in her companion's eyes. 'I'm so sorry...' She searched around in her pockets for a handkerchief—then passed a hand across her cheeks.

'Here.' Taking a handkerchief from his pocket, he gave it to her. 'Come and sit down.' His voice was taut; she glanced up to see the uncontrolled movement of a nerve in the side of his neck. Having settled her comfortably in a chair he went off to get her a drink. On his return he held it out to her.

'What is it?' she quivered, shaking her head. 'I only came to bring your book.' She frowned and gave a sigh. 'I've left it in the basket on my bicycle,' she told him. 'I'll go and fetch it——'

'Sit where you are,' he commanded. 'The book can wait. Drink this; it'll make you feel better.'

'It's brandy,' she said accusingly, and would have pushed it away, but the expression in those grey eyes was warning enough and prudently she took the glass from his hand and put it to her lips.

'Wise girl,' he said tautly. He stood over her for a long silent moment, watching her with the burning liquid, his expression unchanging as she pulled a face with each sip she took. 'Now,' he said at length, 'what's all this about your dismissal?'

'I was expecting it. I told you I was. I didn't know that you had got me the job—at least, I wasn't sure, not until today when Mr Cookson told me. I must admit, though, that I had an idea——'

'Never mind that,' he broke in curtly. 'How did it come about that you received your notice today—I take it you did receive notice?' he added almost harshly. She nodded, suspecting that had Mr Cookson not given her notice, but had instead dismissed her instantly, he would most certainly have heard from Kane. The idea that he would champion her did give a lift to her spirits, but it was not of such magnitude that it showed.

'Yes; he gave me a month's notice, but I shall ask him to release me before that,' she added. 'You see, I've decided to return to England.'

Silence ... so profound and tense that she felt she dared not be the one to break it. Kane seemed to be so deeply involved in some thoughts of his own that he was a million miles away from her.

'You're ... going back to England.' He turned away,

and stood facing the open window, his hands thrust deeply into the pockets of his denims. Lena put down the glass, her eyes never leaving his broad back, silhouetted darkly against the purple twilight which was falling like a gentle cover across the drowsy bushlands. She saw the lights of the native village, the tableau of the mountains, their changeless eminence as awe-inspiring as the timeless veld itself; she saw the line of kopjes, crowned with cacti, the last pearl-grey rays of the sunset fading, low and soft behind them. The silence seemed to sharpen, to hold both Kane and herself in a state of deepest tension and uncertainty. He spoke at last; she knew he was carefully choosing his words as he said, without turning round to face her, 'When are you thinking of going?'

'It'll be best for me to leave as soon after Christmas as possible.' Her voice broke, but she did not think he had noticed. How foolish she had been in falling in love with such a man, she thought as she continued to stare at his back. If she had remained heart-whole then she might have sought for another post and, having settled in it, she would then have begun to find herself a nice little place in which to live.

Well, she realized with a long and shuddering sigh, it was not to be.

'You haven't yet explained how your dismissal came about?' Kane turned at last, his brooding eyes meeting hers and noting the tears that still hung on her lashes.

'It was just a combination of circumstances,' she faltered, troubled as to how she was to keep Magda's name out of this conversation.

His brows lifted interrogatingly.

'What sort of an explanation is that?' he demanded, in the most peremptory tones he had ever used to her.

She averted her head, feeling rather like a child who had been severely admonished.

'I've made several mistakes,' she began, when he interrupted her to say that he was not at all impressed by this kind of admission.

'I shall see Mr Cookson,' he decided.

'Oh ... no! There isn't any reason why you should, Kane.'

His grey eyes were hard, his voice challenging as he asked,

'There isn't? Why?'

Disconcerted by this direct question, she could find nothing to say for a space. Eventually, however, she procrastinated by telling him that it would only embarrass her if he should decide to question Mr Cookson regarding his reason for dismissing her.

'I'd much rather you left things as they are,' she ended, sending him a beseeching glance from under her long silken lashes.

'Probably,' with a hint of asperity, 'but as I am far from convinced that you have made these mistakes you mention I intend to investigate the matter for myself.'

She looked troubled, thinking of his distress when he discovered the perfidy of his girl-friend.

'It really isn't any of your business, Kane,' she said, a hint of apology in her tones.

He lifted an eyebrow, his whole manner one of uncompromising authority.

'On the contrary, it is very much my business. I recommended you for the post and I have a right to know what you did to fail me——'

'Fail!' she broke in before she could prevent herself. 'No, Kane ...' And then her words trailed off to silence as she realized what she had done.

Perceptively he said,

'So you didn't fail me? I didn't for one moment believe that you had.'

She bit her lip, vexed with herself for her impulsiveness.

'It's best that you allow the matter to drop, Kane.'

'Best for whom?' he wanted to know.

She looked directly at him, her gaze clear but troubled.

'For everyone concerned,' she said.

'And what do you mean by "everyone"?' he questioned, causing her to frown and shake her head and accuse him of trying to tie her in knots. 'Nothing of the kind,' he denied in quiet yet authoritative tones. 'I'm merely trying to get some sense out of you. However,' he added with a hint of impatience, 'it doesn't seem as if I'm going to have any success.' He glanced at his watch. 'Come,' he said, 'I'll take you home in the car.'

'In——?' She stared uncomprehendingly at him. 'But why should you?'

He looked at her in some amusement now.

'The answer's simple, Lena. I want to take you home in the car.'

She shook her head, the bewildered expression still in her eyes.

'I don't understand you, Kane,' she told him, a note of complaint in her voice.

His face became tense, unsmiling.

'I don't understand myself,' he responded curtly, and then, noticing that she had emptied her glass, 'Are you ready?'

Meekly she rose, aware that it would be a relief to be taken home in the car.

'It's been so hot and tiring today,' she murmured, scarcely conscious that she spoke aloud.

'It has indeed,' he was swift to agree. 'I shall ask June to see that you go to bed immediately you've had your meal.'

'If you ask me,' said June in a strangely knowing tone of voice, 'there's something mighty interesting afoot tonight.' She and about thirty-five others were the guests of Kane at his Christmas party. It was being held in a large wooden shed which had been originally built for the purpose of entertaining. Dinner had earlier been put on for twenty guests; they were now dancing to recorded music coming from four loud-speakers set up in the corners of the large high building. The remainder of the guests would be arriving shortly, those who preferred to have dinner at home, but who were more than willing to swell the numbers later, when the dancing and the real fun started. For dinner, which had been served in the spacious dining-saloon of Koranna Lodge, they had eaten delicious shrimp *remoulade* followed by salad served in satin-wood bowls. After that, from pewter plates, they had eaten roast turkey with all the trimmings one would find on an English table at Christmastime. Sweets and fruits had followed, all being washed down with excellent wines from Kane's extensive cellar. Coffee and liqueurs had then been taken on the stoep, under shady vines, with coloured fairy-lights interlaced between the foliage. For Lena, who had never experienced anything like it before, it was exciting, as was all that followed afterwards.

She had been dancing with Kane, then with Rex, and now she and June were at the bar. This was a small curving affair made of light-coloured wood. A white-coated servant was there, ready to attend to the requirements of the guests.

'Of course there's something interesting afoot,' agreed Lena in response to her friend's declaration. 'The whole thing's interesting. I've never seen anything so lavish in my life.'

'It's lavish enough. I wasn't thinking of the party

itself, though. It's—well—something in the air, if you know what I mean?'

'Something in the air?'

June nodded, but now seemed reluctant to add to what she had said. However, up came Rex with the news, given *sotto voce* as he stooped and put his head between the faces of the two girls,

'It's rumoured that Kane's going to announce his engagement tonight!'

'He's...?' Lena's heart turned painfully. 'Who—who told you, Rex?' She had to sound calm, interested, but not too interested. She hoped she was not as white as she felt, hoped the trembling sensation within her was not reflected in any nervous movement of a nerve or muscle.

'It's all over the place. Murmurings and whisperings; looks and stares in Magda's direction. Expectancy—all the guests at fever pitch as they wait for the great announcement!'

Lena turned her head, to find Kane and Magda. He had danced with the girl several times already, but he was not with her now. She was dancing with Stephen, and the last dance had been with Phil Thorsby. Where was Kane?

'Come and dance with me,' invited Rex, and as Gerald came at that particular moment to claim his wife for the waltz, Lena went off with Rex.

'I hear you're leaving the shop,' he said after a hesitant moment. 'Is it true?'

Lena nodded and said yes, it was true.

'I'm going home after Christmas,' she added.

'You are?' Rex held her from him. 'I'm sorry to hear that, Lena. I feel as if we might have got to know each other a lot better, given time.'

Faintly she smiled.

'I feel obliged to return to England,' she said. Only

three days ago she had had word from Mrs Poulton, saying definitely that she could not have the children, but pointing out that, put into care, they could be separated. They would most certainly be unhappy, she had ended as a parting shot.

'For any particular reason?' inquired Rex. 'I mean, I'd understood from Gerald that there really wasn't any necessity for you to return, as you're quite alone in the world?'

'I have three young stepbrothers,' she told him.

'You have——?' Rex broke off as the music stopped. Lena managed to escape, relieved that he had not been given the opportunity of asking any further questions.

She looked around, saw Kane, immaculate and inordinately attractive in a white tropical suit, his skin bronzed and shining, his hair, thick and wavy, brushed back from his low, aristocratic forehead. His eyes lighting on her, he smiled and came right across the floor towards where she stood, a trifle pale, her heart still unsteady from the news which Rex had just a short while ago imparted.

'Dance with me,' said Kane imperiously, taking her arm before she could speak.

She danced close to him, savouring every precious second—because before very long her heart would be breaking. How could she stand there, with the other guests—all of them so gay and happy—and listen to the announcement of Kane's engagement to Magda? How could she join those who, crowding round the happy pair to congratulate them, offered sincere wishes for their future happiness.

'I will not,' she cried to herself vehemently. 'I will not stay and witness the scene!' She would say she was feeling off colour. Yes, that was it! Gerald would drive her home and then come back. It wouldn't take him more than a few minutes . . .

'May I say how very lovely you look tonight, Lena?' The soft voice broke into her plan and she gave a small start. She looked up, her eyes shadowed so deeply that a sudden frown appeared between his eyes.

'Thank you, Kane.'

'Your hair suits you this way.'

'Thank you, Kane.'

'Did you make this dress yourself?'

'Yes.'

'It's delightful.'

'Thank you, Kane.'

'Can't you think of anything else to say?' he laughed.

'There are times,' she said, 'when you can't think of eloquent things to say.' She felt so depressed now that she scarcely cared if he knew.

'There's a vast division between eloquence and repetition.'

'I don't feel like talking, Kane.' She raised her eyes to his, missed a step and fell against him. 'I—I don't feel very well . . .' This was sheer cowardice. She must stay, must be there to offer him her good wishes. After all, he had been her friend almost from the time she arrived here. He had saved her life and thought nothing of it; he had stocked the garden she was making; he had spoken for her with Mr Cookson, making sure she was given the job . . . Lena's thoughts trailed off, but took another line almost immediately. *Why* should Kane have helped her so much with the garden? *Why* had he lent her the pony? In fact, why had he done anything for her at all?

'You don't feel well? Lena—this is the third time I've asked you that question!' He stopped, and held her from him, his keen eyes making a thorough examination of her face.

'Oh, is it?' she faltered. 'I'm so sorry, Kane, I'm

afraid I was miles away.'

'Are you unwell?' he asked even yet again.

'No—er...'

'You're certainly not too happy?'

'I expect it's the idea of going home. You always feel a little down when a holiday's coming to an end.'

He said nothing, but before she knew what his intentions were she was outside, in the splendour of his lovely garden, with the scent of flowers assailing her nostrils.

'I have something to ask you,' he said when she would have spoken. 'But we'll move away from the lights and the noise.' There was a sort of new resolution about him, an air of content, as if he were viewing a decision judiciously made.

'I don't understand,' she began. 'Is it important?'

'Very important.'

'Oh,' she murmured, because there was nothing else she could think of to say.

'It's the most important question I shall ask in the whole of my life.' He was increasing his pace. Breathlessly she trotted along at his side. And then he stopped suddenly, and looked down into her lovely face. 'Have you no idea what the question is?' he asked in tones so tender that her heart actually leapt right up into her throat. 'If you haven't my love, then you're ridiculously obtuse.'

'My love...' She stared into his eyes as one fascinated. 'You said—you said——' The rest was smothered by his kiss as, having taken her into his arms even while she was stammering out her words, he bent his head, to seek and find her lips.

'My dear little love,' he murmured presently, his lips close to her cheek. 'You reciprocate divinely.'

She blushed enchantingly at his words, her mind still dazed, and yet she was thinking of the questions she had only recently been asking herself, as she danced close to Kane, savouring the feel of his arms about her. She had wondered why he should have taken such an interest in her, why he had done so much for her. And now so many other incidents passed, one after another, through her mind. Those times when she had sensed a struggle within him, when he had been so concerned that she should not have the children ... oh, there was a whole string of pointers—if only she had been quick enough to have seen them.

'You didn't want to fall in love with me, did you?' she just had to say when, a long while later, they were sitting close together by the stream, listening to the clear crystal water cascading over the rocks.

'I didn't want to fall in love with anybody,' he was honest enough to admit, 'but with you, my dearest, I was fighting a losing battle from the start.'

'Magda,' she murmured. 'Everyone believed you'd marry her——' She stopped, for a fleeting moment experiencing the agony she had known on hearing Rex say that the announcement of Kane's engagement to Magda would probably be made tonight.

'Magda,' he said, and there was nothing in his voice but indifference, 'never meant anything to me at all. She's good company, but not the kind of girl for me. I love nature and natural things. I happen to love a girl who is natural, a girl who doesn't know the meaning of the word affectation.' Because he knew she would be embarrassed by this flattery he drew her close and kissed her tenderly on the lips. 'I expect it was your love of nature which attracted me in the first place. You see, my darling, I hadn't ever met anyone like you before.' He sounded almost humble, she thought, and wondered where was the austerity, the arrogance which June had so often mentioned. It was still there, and always would be. It was a part of him ... but a part which she herself would rarely see. 'Do you remember my saying that a person's character shapes his or her destiny?'

'Yes, I remember.' Lena leant away, and looked inquiringly at him, her eyes and her hair and her face glowing in the moonlight. 'I didn't know what you meant.'

'I meant that, as your character is what others like or dislike, it either repels or attracts. In my case it attracted.'

'I remember wondering if you were telling me you liked me,' she said with a shy smile. 'I see now that you were.'

Kane nodded his head.

'And I must have known then that I was well on my way to falling in love with you, simply because the attraction I spoke of was in fact going to shape your destiny.'

'Because I was to become your wife?'

'Of course,' with a return of that arrogance she knew so well. However, the next moment he was asking her, in the most tender tone he knew, if she would marry him.

'I can't believe it,' she said, drawing a deep breath. 'You see, Kane, I was expecting you to announce your engagement to Magda tonight.'

'You—what!' Kane had been about to draw her close again, but instead he pulled away, staring at her in the moonlight, amazement looking out from his eyes. 'Where on earth did you get an idea like that?'

'It was a rumour that was going round.'

'Rubbish! How could it?'

Lena explained what Rex had said. She also mentioned the bracelet and earrings, this latter coming out involuntarily, as if it just had to be said.

Again amazement looked out of Kane's eyes.

'You mean—that people believed I'd actually made Magda a gift of that jewellery?' And, when Lena nodded, 'She had sent it to Johannesburg to be cleaned, and to have some minor repairs done to it. As I was going there she asked if I'd pick it up. Magda is the very last girl I'd buy jewellery for,' he added grimly.

'You only collected it for her?' Lena could not help recalling the heartache that jewellery had caused her. For it seemed so feasible that, if Kane had bought it for her, then he must be seriously considering marrying her. 'I wonder how a rumour like that got around?'

'It's not difficult to guess at its origin,' was Kane's contemptuous reply, and as Lena knew that he was referring to Magda herself she said nothing. She was not interested in the girl any more. And yet, after a sweet and tender interlude during which Kane's passionate kisses left her gasping for breath, she did bring up the girl's name again, asking if, on that occasion when Magda had been arguing with Lena over the date on which the book was supposed to have arrived, Kane had come to her, Lena, in order to comfort her.

'I felt that you believed me, even though Mr Cookson didn't,' she added, nestling close to his breast.

'I knew at once that you were speaking the truth,' he returned without hesitation. 'Your frank and honest expression was more than enough to convince me of who was in the wrong. Yes, my love, I did come to comfort you, and I should have known then that my battle was hopelessly lost—just as I should have known it that day when we were at the waterfall. I can't think now how I managed to resist taking you in my arms.'

'I felt there was something,' she murmured, still close to his breast. But after a while Kane held her from him; she saw the light of tender amusement that lit his dark grey eyes.

'I'd enjoyed my bachelor state so long that I naturally fought to retain it,' he admitted ruefully. 'Marriage had no appeal for me ... not until you came, my beloved. But when you did appear, it was the beginning of the end for me.' Gently he brought her to him again, seeking her lips and taking them possessively. Breathless when at last she was released, she looked lovingly into his eyes and said, a tremor of emotion in her voice,

'I was so miserable, Kane, because I had discovered that I loved you, and I thought I had no chance. But I see now that I ought to have realized the significance of all those things you did for me.'

'I'm sorry, my darling, if I made you unhappy by my tardiness. And even now, I wonder if I'd still be holding on to my freedom if it hadn't been for the fact of your determination to leave here.'

She looked up at him.

'You mean—it was owing to my dismissal that you made up your mind?'

He nodded his head.

'I knew I couldn't let you go.' He paused a moment and she wondered what he was thinking about. She was soon to know, for he told her that he had seen Mr Cookson and after learning of the circumstances leading to her dismissal had known instantly that Magda had been responsible for bringing it about. 'She defeated herself,' he went on with a grim note to his voice. 'It would appear that she would have liked to marry me; it was also a fact that she was jealous of you. She determined to bring about your dismissal, concluding that you would then be forced to leave Africa. But it was the fact that you were intending to leave that brought me to my senses.'

So Magda's scheming had rebounded upon herself, mused Lena, and because she was only human—and all woman besides—she could not help feeling rather exultant at the vision of Magda's face when she learned that Kane was going to marry the girl she had so detested. Kane was talking again, admitting that he had begun to suspect that Lena was falling in love with him and, because of his determination to fight shy of marriage, he had given Magda rather more of his attention than he otherwise would have done. Hence the rumour which had caused Lena so much heartache.

'I suppose I was hoping you would find someone else,' he confessed ruefully. 'Rex, for instance.'

She could not help saying,

'You were sarcastic about Rex's attention on a couple of occasions.'

'I was jealous of him. You know darned well I was!'

'I do now, but I didn't at the time.'

'Then you were a blind little idiot!' But his eyes were tenderer than his tone and within seconds she was drawn closely into his strong arms, and they stayed together like this, listening to the night sounds of the forest and the veld. Above the rhythm of the stream was the incessant whirr of the cicadas; in the distance there was the hollow echo of a night-bird, and from the direction of the village there drifted the primeval sound of a drum-beat. 'My dearest love,' murmured Kane at last, 'we must return to our guests.'

'*Our* guests...' Lena turned in his arms, a deep sigh of contentment escaping her. 'That sounds wonderful, Kane.'

'I shall announce our engagement as soon as we get in,' he told her decisively. 'Can you imagine just what a sensation we're about to cause, my love?' he added with a laugh.

She nodded, thinking of Jennifer, who was in there now, dancing. Earlier she had looked at the shining Magda and frowningly confessed to Lena that she did not care whom her cousin married so long as it was not the girl everyone expected him to marry.

'I must admit,' Lena was saying as she and Kane strolled, hand in hand, back to the shed, 'that I'll be glad when the actual announcement's over and done with.'

'You're not scared?' he protested. 'It'll be a one-minute wonder, but after that everyone will be telling me what a lucky man I am.'

It was to transpire that these confident predictions were correct. It was also to transpire that Magda, when at last she was able to believe her ears, was immediately to collect her coat and leave the party, fury and frustration raging deep within her. However, the couple outside in the garden did not know this yet as, strolling hand in hand, their minds totally occupied with each other and the love they were to share, they stopped now and then to kiss, and to murmur words of endearment to one another, while all around them was the heady perfume of a myriad exotic flowers while, beyond these lovely gardens, there lay the silent bushveld, spreading in hushed and mystic silence towards the dark and distant eminence of the mountains.

Dear Reader,

We at Mills & Boon are only too well aware of the burden of price increases that everyone is having to bear in the present economic situation. So we are constantly looking for new ways to make economies in the production of our books which can help us to maintain our present prices.

Nevertheless we are faced with ever-increasing costs of printing, paper and handling.

In order to avoid passing on the latest round of increases to you, the reader, we have decided to use a slightly thinner paper for our romances, beginning with the April titles. This will make only a small difference to the thickness of each paperback; there will, of course, still be a full 192 pages of romance in each book.

This small change will enable us to keep the price of our paperback romances to 30p and we hope it will help you to enjoy more of the romance reading you know you can rely on.

Yours sincerely,

MILLS & BOON